FACE TO FACE

FACE ▶ TO ◀ FACE

A Novel by
MARION DANE BAUER

CLARION BOOKS ▪ NEW YORK

Clarion Books
a Houghton Mifflin Company imprint
215 Park Avenue South, New York, NY 10003
Text copyright © 1991 by Marion Dane Bauer

Printed in the USA.

Library of Congress Cataloging-in-Publication Data
Bauer, Marion Dane.
  Face to face / by Marion Dane Bauer.
    p.   cm.
  Summary: Picked on at school by bullies, thirteen-year-
old Michael confronts his fears during a trip to Colorado to
see his father, who works as a whitewater rafting guide and
whom Michael has not seen in eight years.
  ISBN 0–395–55440–3
  [1. Fear—Fiction.   2. Fathers and sons—Fiction.
3. Rafting (Sports)—Fiction.]   I. Title.
PZ7.B3262Fac   1991
[Fic]—dc20   90–49608
                                               CIP
                                                AC

MP   10   9   8   7   6   5   4   3   2   1

For now we see through a glass, darkly . . .

1 Corinthians 13:12

Acknowledgments

My thanks to David and Ralph Johnston and to Twyla
Thorson and Tenus and Lola Thorson, of Houston,
Minnesota, who shared their dairy farms with me.

To Carol Gardener and to Kevin Kahalin, who guided
me safely through the whitewater rapids of Brown's
Canyon and the Royal Gorge.

To JoAnn Bren Guernsey and to Emily Crofford, who
listened, advised, encouraged through every draft.

To my editor, James Cross Giblin, who gave patience
and wisdom, as always.

And my deepest thanks to Ann Goddard, who accom-
panied every journey this story required.

For my son,
Peter Dane Bauer,
with love and admiration

■ ■ ■ ■ ■

FACE TO FACE

It was the same dream again. Michael knew it was a dream, even as the rage swelled, almost smothering the terror pounding in his chest.

The nightmare usually started off so innocently. He might be playing three-man baseball with Gary and Chris behind Gary's barn. Or hiking in the wooded hills surrounding his farm. Or doing chores. Once he had been in church, listening to one of Pastor Johnston's terminally boring sermons. Or not exactly listening. Even in the dream, the pastor's voice had been a kind of soothing backdrop for Michael's own thoughts. And then, inevitably, but completely unexpectedly, the explosions always began.

This time, though, everything was different, because he had known from the beginning it was *that* dream. This time he was in school, which was where the real event had occurred. It was the last moment of the final day of seventh grade. He was careening through the halls, rejoicing . . . blissfully unaware of the string of tiny firecrackers dangling from the back pocket of his jeans or of the barest suggestion of a flame that was licking along the fuse.

Michael watched his dream self, vulnerable, unsuspecting. Watched that other Michael toss a book into the air and catch it again. But he could find no way to warn him.

Even seeing it all from far off — because though he was still himself in the school hallway, he also watched everything from above — he never got a chance to see who had lit the firecrackers and stuffed them into his pocket. He knew who it was he suspected, but he was never able to make out any particular face. And despite the fact that he should have been prepared by now, when the firecrackers began to go off, there he was again. Whirling in confusion and panic. Dancing to the sizzling explosions that seemed to be happening inside his own skull.

When the string of firecrackers had played itself out, leaving his ears ringing and a pulsing burn in the small of his back, the laughter took over where the explosions had been. His tormenters surrounded him, every one of them bigger than he, taller and stronger, too. And they opened their mouths like dank caves, roaring laughter.

"Look at wittle Mikey!" they called to one another. "Is him scared?"

Then, abruptly, the dream changed, as it always did. And Michael found himself standing apart from his tormenters, apart even from his friends. Facing them all. Holding his new bolt-action .22 rifle. He nestled it into his shoulder, laid his cheek against the satiny stock, and began to fire. Deliberately. Accurately. And one by one, the faces exploded in front of him. One by one, they dissolved. Disappeared. Died.

Until only Michael was left, holding his gun. Until in all the world there was only Michael Ostrom.

Each time when he awakened, victorious but in a trembling sweat, Michael found himself sitting up in bed, his hands still curved around the nonexistent rifle . . . weeping.

The alarm beside his bed racketed wildly, and Michael slammed a hand down on it, tipping it over instead of turning it off. It was an old-fashioned windup clock that Dave had "loaned" him years ago when Michael had sometimes gone back to sleep after his mother had called him for morning chores. Now he would rather have had a clock radio, but it hadn't been an item on his list for today, his thirteenth birthday. There had been only one thing on that list.

A .22 rifle.

Michael sat up, righted the shrieking clock, and connected with the knob on the top this time. His sheet and light summer blanket were in disarray, half spilled onto the floor.

He'd had the dream again last night. The nightmare. He shivered and pulled up the sheet to cover himself, though the morning was warm even for mid-June in Minnesota.

The worst part of the whole thing was that the dream never changed, that it came out the same way every time. First the firecrackers. His own embarrassed terror. Then the fierce need to destroy, to kill everyone within range. When he found himself standing there with the gleaming new rifle in his hands, beyond fear, beyond even rage . . . it all seemed so inevitable.

Almost as though he had no choice.

Why did the dream keep coming back? Having lit firecrackers stuffed into his pocket in the school hallway had been embarrassing. There was no question about that. And scary, too, at least until he had realized what was going on. But it had only been a culmination of all the other "jokes" he had been enduring this whole past year in junior high. And school had been out for two weeks now. All that was over, at least for the summer.

He didn't know why the bullies had chosen him, anyway . . . except that he was small for his age, had always been small but seemed to have gotten smaller lately in relation to his classmates. Most of the seventh-grade girls were bigger than he was. And once you got to junior high, not having a physique like an ape seemed to be some kind of crime. Even a few of the kids from his own grade school, like Neil Hansen, who was just a year ahead of him and lived on the next farm down the road, had gotten into the teasing. In fact, Michael was almost certain Neil had put the firecrackers in his back pocket.

Guys like Neil would think twice about messing with him when they found out that he had a .22.

Not that he would shoot anybody, like in the dream.

All he wanted was to own the gun, to feel the weight of it in his hands, to see the respect that would come into the bullies' eyes. But he had no intention of hurting anybody, really.

His father used to say — his real father, not Dave — that you didn't shoot anything unless you intended to eat it. Except for varmints, rats around the barn or the ever-present pigeons. Even Neil Hansen probably wouldn't qualify as a varmint.

"Happy birthday, Michael!" His mother appeared in the doorway of his bedroom.

Michael nodded sleepily and tried on a smile. It felt strange on his face, as though it didn't fit.

"Are you up?" she asked cheerfully, though it was obvious he wasn't.

He put his feet on the floor. "I don't have to wait until supper for my gift, do I? Couldn't I open it right after breakfast?" He said *gift* instead of *gifts*. Rifles were expensive. If he got it, there wouldn't be anything else.

If he got it — the thought was like an icy breeze along his skin — there wouldn't be anything more he would want. Except maybe . . . But no, some things were too much even to dream. Certainly too much to expect to have delivered for your birthday.

His mom didn't like guns, but she was on his side about having one, anyway. She knew how important it was to him. Dave didn't like guns either. Dave was his mother's husband. The law said that marrying Michael's mother and signing some adoption papers in front of a judge made him Michael's father as well. As if a few papers could erase Michael's real father from the face of the earth.

Mom was smiling and shaking her head, her dark, blunt-cut hair swinging. "Supper has always been the time for presents, Michael . . . after the cake."

Michael groaned, though he had known that was what she would say.

"I came to ask what you would like for your birthday breakfast," she added, as if anything she might fix for breakfast could make up for his having to wait through the entire day to get his gun.

He shrugged, but then he said anyway, knowing it was what she wanted to hear, "How about Belgian waffles?"

"With fresh strawberries? And whipped cream?"

"And sausage. The patty kind, not links."

His mother nodded, obviously pleased. She loved cooking, especially anything a little different, and the first time she had used her new Belgian waffle maker, Michael had eaten seven fat, crisp waffles, one after the other. Such a response or any kind of special request was, for her, like applause to a singer. "When you go out to the barn, tell your father I'll be there in a few minutes. That's a yeast batter. I'll need to get it started before I come."

He's not my father, Michael wanted to remind her, but of course, he didn't. Those words had never been spoken in this house. Instead he got up and pulled on his jeans. His mother hovered there in the doorway, as though there was something else she wanted to say. But after a moment she smiled again, a little more tentatively this time, and turned to go downstairs. It had been that way a lot lately, almost as if she was scared . . . of him. Sometimes he couldn't help wondering if she knew about his dream.

But that was silly. No one, not even a mother, could read your dreams unless you told what they were. And he hadn't told her or anyone else . . . except for his father. His real father. They had talked about it, the way they talked about everything in Michael's life. It didn't matter that the conversations happened only in Michael's thoughts. They were still real.

His father had told him not to feel bad about the gun, about what he had done. It was only a dream, after all.

Michael pulled on socks and headed to the bathroom. His barn shirt and boots were waiting in the small porch off the kitchen. His mother was adamant about boots worn in the barn never coming into the house. Even so, it was almost impossible to keep the smell of the barn out entirely. Everything on the place, indoors and out, seemed to absorb the rich, warm fragrance of hay and manure.

Michael didn't mind the smell. Actually, he found it almost comforting, reminiscent of the barn's golden warmth and the steamy companionship of cattle. Still, since he had begun junior high, he was always careful to keep his barn clothes separated from anything he wore to school. He even made a point, on school mornings, to start chores early enough to be sure he had time to shower as well as change before he caught the bus.

In grade school such things hadn't mattered so much. Most of the kids at the small school in Eleva came from farms. In the consolidated junior high, however, there were more town kids. And they made fun of the ones who came to school with the slightest hint of chores clinging to their skin or clothes.

Town kids didn't have chores to do. Feed the cat, maybe. Take out the garbage. Big deal. Still, Michael wouldn't trade with any of them. He loved the farm, the animals, even the constant routine of the work. It was as reliable as the seasons, something that could be counted on in a way nothing they taught in school could.

He descended the stairs two at a time, pausing just long enough to gulp a glass of orange juice his mother had set out on the table for him. He had been daw-dling, and probably even Kari, his five-year-old sister — half sister, actually, because Dave was her father — would be at work already.

"I know. I'm late," he said to his mother, plunking the glass on the table. "But don't worry. When I get out there, I'm going to work like ten people."

"That I'd like to see," she said, though she said it pleasantly enough. She was referring to the fact that he was noted for being caught dreaming in the midst of chores, leaning on a pitchfork or against the warm flank of a cow, his thoughts caught in a time warp. "Just keep it calm around the ladies. Okay?"

The ladies was what she called their dairy herd. Her dairy herd, really, because she had inherited this farm from her parents. And she had a personal relationship with her cows, all 138 of them, every one of which she had named at birth. Many of the farmers these days identified their cows only by registration numbers, but his mother named each of theirs, even the bull calves they kept only until they were market weight.

"I'll keep it calm," he called from the porch, pulling on his boots and reaching for his shirt. "A fast calm." And he poked his head back into the kitchen to grin at his mother before he pushed out the screen door.

Nipper, their aging lab-shepherd mix, came to greet Michael, which meant that the first of the cows were already in the barn and settled into their stalls. That was Nipper's job, helping bring the cows in when the weather was good enough for them to be pastured between milkings, and the old dog seemed to exist for the privilege of performing it.

Nipper thrust his grizzled muzzle into Michael's hand. *Where were you?* he was saying, but it was only a question, not a criticism. His entire back half moved with his welcoming tail.

"Is Kari already out there feeding the calves?" Michael asked, and the tail went harder. She undoubtedly was. She was almost as enthusiastic about her chores as Nipper was about his.

Dave looked up from the far end of the barn when Michael came through the door, but he didn't say anything. Even when Michael called, "Mom'll be here in a few minutes. She's starting the batter for Belgian waffles," he still made no comment.

That's the way it usually was. Dave chose his words as though there were a limited supply and the few he had been given had to be made to last. He hardly needed to speak, though. The very curve of his back as he bent over to attach a milking machine spoke for him.

What's been keeping you? his burly back seemed to say. *Look how far along I am with the chores.*

But then it was always like that. Nothing Michael ever did, nothing he could be was good enough for this man.

Michael set to work. "Hi, Rilda," he said, reaching for a rag in a disinfectant solution, ready and waiting for him there. He squatted to wash the cow's udder in preparation for the milking machine, speaking in a low, soothing voice.

Rilda was a red-and-white Guernsey, the only red they had in a herd of black-and-whites. And she belonged to Michael. Dave had been trying for several years to breed one like her, and then the first time a yet-to-be-born calf was assigned to Michael, he'd gotten lucky.

Michael had expected Dave to claim her, at least to trade her for a black-and-white, but he hadn't. "A deal's a deal," he'd said. But that was all. Not a word about Michael's luck . . . or all his work that followed. He hadn't even congratulated Michael when Rilda had won a trophy at the county fair or when she had brought down a blue ribbon at state. Not that Michael cared.

"Today's my birthday," Michael told Rilda softly, "and I'm going to get a bolt-action .22." He brushed his forehead lightly against her flank. "It's going to be just like the one my dad used to — "

"Michael."

Michael looked up, startled to see Dave looming above him.

"Is Rilda the only one you're milking this morning, or had you planned on one or two more?" Dave's voice was quiet, his blue eyes and square jaw impassive, but the words cut like knives. He picked up the brush he had come for and returned to the other end of the barn without waiting for any kind of reply.

Michael's face flamed. He straightened up and threw the rag at the bucket. It missed and landed on the barn floor, which meant he would have to go after a fresh cloth before he could prepare the next cow.

He couldn't stand it any longer! Everywhere he turned there was someone pushing him around. Stuffing his pockets with firecrackers.

When he went to get the milking machine down from its hook, he discovered he was trembling all over the way he always did when he woke from the dream.

·2·

Michael watched Kari. She was cutting with meticulous care along the ridge of a square of waffle, intent on preserving the tiny puddle of syrup inside the square. Her tousled blond curls almost vibrated with her concentration.

She looked up, apparently feeling the weight of Michael's gaze, and regarded him solemnly. "It's your birthday," she told him, as if he might not know. She was like that, quiet like her father and almost too serious for a little kid. When she spoke it was with the authority of someone much older than five.

"Yeah," Michael agreed. "I'm a big teenager now. That means nobody can push me around anymore. Right?"

The joke fell flat. Kari's blue eyes remained serious, and she didn't reply. She seemed to be considering whether it might be true that he had grown beyond being pushed around. Michael returned his attention to the waffle on his own plate.

"The alfalfa in the north field is ready to cut," Dave said, forking another sausage from the platter. "Can you take care of that today, Michael?"

"Yeah . . . sure," Michael replied, letting the sullenness that had become his trademark with Dave slide into his voice. Actually, he loved haying. It gave him a chance to drive the tractor, though only the small John Deere. Dave didn't let him do anything with the big, new Versatile. Still, he wasn't going to pretend the man was doing him some kind of favor, handing out assignments the way he did.

Dave acted as though the farm was his instead of being something he had married into. He was the youngest of four sons, so he hadn't had a chance at his parents' farm. Michael had heard some of the older guys talking, those who were younger sons in farm families. They drove about the countryside checking out places with expensive silos . . . and daughters, planning how they could marry themselves a good farm.

Before he had married Michael's mother, Dave hadn't farmed for years. He had worked in the feed store in Eleva. Except for the time he'd spent in Vietnam.

Michael had been seven years old when his mother and Dave got married, and he had sworn to himself, standing beside the new couple in the small Lutheran church in Eleva, that Dave would never take his father's place. And he never had, even though Michael hadn't seen his father for nearly eight years now.

There had been times when Michael had come close to forgetting his vow. Like when he had cut his leg open pulling a tangle of heavy weeds out of the sickle in the hay bind. Dave had scooped him into his arms and run from the field all the way to the house, then driven him to the emergency room in a blur of rare speed.

Something always came along, though, to save him from forgetting. Like Dave's standing by his hospital bed afterwards, unable to find a single thing to say. Not, "I'm sorry you got hurt." Not, "You were brave not to cry through all those stitches." Not even, "I hope you get well soon, son." He had never called him *son*, for that matter, and Michael was glad. He had never called Dave *Dad*, either.

And then there had been the time, just this past winter, when Michael had picked a fight with Neil Hansen, expecting Dave's help. Dave had been standing right by the mailbox when the school bus had pulled up, and Neil, obviously not noticing Dave there, had decided to get off at Michael's stop.

Michael hadn't needed to wait to see what Neil had in mind. He'd had his face washed with snow more than once by the big bully, usually before an appreciative audience. And as the bus pulled away, Michael decided that he was going to turn the tables this time. There was help at hand, after all. Dave could have picked Neil up and shaken him like a puppy.

But he didn't. He hadn't lifted a finger to interfere. When Michael threw himself at Neil, a fistful of snow in each hand, Dave didn't even yell at them to stop the way any other adult would have. He just stood there, watching. At least Michael supposed he must have watched.

Neil had taken charge immediately, grabbing

Michael by both wrists before he could even release his missiles, twisting his arms behind his back until there had been no choice but to drop the loose snow. Then Neil had taken him by the scruff of the neck and ground his face into the icy gravel, holding him down until the road slush had begun to melt and run in cold rivulets down Michael's cheeks.

Only then, after Neil had swaggered off down the road, did Dave find the time or the inclination to stroll over and give Michael a hand. Just one hand. In the other he held the precious mail he had come to collect.

"You bit off more than you could chew that time," was all Dave said. But his face had said the rest for him. His face had said that he couldn't figure out how he ever came to be connected with such a scrawny, useless kid.

For Michael, it had been the last straw. His mother had been telling him for years that he needed to give Dave a chance, and look what Dave's "chance" had brought him!

Now Michael sighed and put down his fork, his second waffle only half eaten. Usually he ate enormous quantities, despite his size, but some days sitting at the table with Dave made swallowing hard.

"May I be excused?" he asked, and his mother arched one eyebrow at him inquisitively.

"Is that all you want?"

"Yeah. I'm not very — " But the telephone rang, saving him from further explanations. "I'll get it," he said instead and jumped up. Maybe it would be Gary. If

Michael got right to the haying, there might still be time for them to mess around a while in the afternoon before chores.

When he picked up the phone there was, at first, a low hum on the line, and he could hear someone in the background, talking and laughing. "Hello," he said.

There was no answer.

"Hello?" he repeated.

"Mike?" the distant voice said at last. "Is that you?"

"Yeah," Michael replied tentatively. No one called him Mike. Not even his friends. It just didn't fit, somehow. Maybe this was a wrong number.

And then the voice began to sing "Happy Birthday to You." Michael stood with the receiver in his hand, not knowing what to do . . . or say. It must be some kind of joke. Should he hang up? Whatever came next would probably be unpleasant.

"Who is it?" his mother was asking in the background. But Michael just shrugged and turned his back to his family, holding the strange voice away from all of them. Who would call him on a line that sounded as though it passed under the sea and sing that dumb birthday song?

"You know who this is, don't you, Mike?" the voice asked when the song was over. "Can't you guess?"

"No," he replied, impatient now. His skin prickled with foreboding, but he couldn't have named the bad thing he imagined coming next.

"The last time I saw you, you were about the size of a peanut. I'll bet you're a big, strapping fellow now."

Michael stared at the slim, white phone on the wall as if he could see through it to the other end of the line. The only person he could think of, the only person he *wanted* to think of . . . but it couldn't be. Could it?

"Um . . . um . . . Dad?" he inquired in a voice squeezed of air. Behind him his mother let out a small, wordless exclamation, and Michael stepped closer to the wall, lowering his head and cradling the receiver protectively against his shoulder. "Is that you?"

"You've got it!" came the shout, thin and distant. "I knew you'd remember!"

Remember! How could anybody on earth forget his own father? "Yeah," he said. "Sure. I mean . . . how are you?"

"How am I? Fine. Never been better."

Something inside Michael sank. What was the matter? Did he want his father to be calling because he was sick or in trouble? Of course not. Maybe, though, he wanted him to be missing him, and feeling the missing, just a bit. The way Michael had missed his father every single day since he had gone.

"Good," Michael told him. "That's good."

"Maybe you'd better ask *where* I am. Where I've been."

"Where are you?" Michael asked, obediently. He still hadn't the slightest idea what this conversation was about.

"Well, I've been lots of places. Flown mail and supply planes in Alaska. Dusted crops in the Dakotas. Unloaded those big ships in San Francisco. But right now . . . you'll never guess."

Michael figured he wouldn't, so he didn't try.

"Right now I'm in the Rockies . . . in Colorado," his father said. "I'm a guide for a whitewater rafting company."

"Whitewater rafting?" Michael drew in his breath. "I've always wanted to do that!"

"Really?"

"Yeah!" Actually, he had never given much thought to whitewater rafting until this very minute. But the instant his father mentioned it, he knew he would prefer charging through the rapids of a mountain river to any other activity on earth. "It must be lots of fun."

"Well, it is, I can tell you. And in fact, that's what I called about. I thought maybe you'd like to come out here for a visit this summer. All you have to do is fly into Denver and I can pick you up there. Any day. You name it."

Tomorrow! Michael wanted to shout. *I'll be there tomorrow . . . first thing!* But he knew better than that. His mother and Dave might not even let him go. A dairy farm demanded every member of the family, especially in the summer when there were crops to deal with as well as the stock. Not to mention that this was his father Michael would be asking to see. His mother rarely said anything about her first husband, good or bad, but Michael had learned long ago not to bring him up as a subject of conversation.

Still they had to let him go. They just had to!

Michael pressed his forehead into the mushroom design of the wallpaper in front of him and said, in a voice that came out smaller than he intended, "I'll have to ask."

"You do that, Mike. You ask. Here. Let me give you my number. It's the office number for an outfit called River Rafters in Salida. You can call them and leave a message for Bert, that's me, any time during business hours. Then I'll call you back."

"Okay." Numbly Michael picked up the pencil that hung by a string from the telephone message pad. "Go ahead."

His father gave him the number, and Michael wrote it down, repeating it twice to make sure he had it right. Then the conversation was over, and he was standing with the receiver in his hand, a sharp buzz swarming at the edge of his awareness.

He hung up the phone, finally, and turned to face his family. His mother and Kari and Dave, sitting at the table on the other side of the room, looked back at him.

"That was my dad," he said, though he knew they had already guessed. A glance flew between his mother and Dave like a storm-flung cloud. "He called to wish me a happy birthday."

No one spoke, but they were each clearly waiting for more. Even Kari.

"He's living in Colorado now, guiding white-water raft trips, and he wants me to come visit him." Michael said it all in a rush, as if the idea could be scurried past them without their quite noticing what it was.

"For heaven's sake!" His mother balled her paper napkin and threw it down next to her plate. Her cheeks were flushed. "Why would Bert Hensley decide to start interfering now?"

"He's not interfering, Mom. He wants me. That's all." And then Michael added, more softly but very definitely, "And I want to go."

Dave said nothing. It was one time, however, when Michael didn't object to the man's silence. Dave could stay out of this entirely as far as he was concerned.

"Please, Mom. Please?" Michael took a step toward the table, then stopped, his hands clasped in a gesture that might have been prayer.

His mother looked at Dave, apparently trying to read his reaction to all of this. Not that Michael could see anything there to read. She spoke without taking her eyes from her husband's face.

"You're needed here, Michael. You know that." There was something in her voice that didn't seem to be heading toward a refusal, though — not a firm one, anyway.

Michael squeezed his hands together until the knuckles turned pearly. "It's not forever," he pleaded. "I'll be back. And when I come back, I'll work twice as hard. I promise."

His mother hesitated. She pushed her hair behind one ear on the side where it always fell forward into her face. "I'm going to let your father decide," she said.

"My father?" Michael stared at her, uncomprehending. But almost instantly he realized his mistake. His mother meant Dave. Of course. "Oh." He turned limply to Dave.

Dave's pale blue eyes were bottomless.

Michael bit his lower lip.

Dave stood, and at first Michael thought he was going to walk out without saying a word, leaving everyone else to fill in the blanks. Instead, he picked up his dishes and carried them to the kitchen sink as he always did after a meal. Then he rinsed the plate, placed it carefully in the dishwasher, and did the same with his coffee cup and silverware. After he had straightened up he announced, finally, "I'll have to think about it."

Michael remained where he was standing, still rigid. When Dave had gone outside and closed the door behind himself, Michael released his bottom lip from between his tightly clenched teeth and licked away the slight taste of blood he found there.

For nearly eight years, he had waited for his father to come home. Even after his mother had remarried, even after Michael had grown old enough to know that there was no hope, he had gone on waiting. That he could be invited to go to his father instead had never occurred to him. Not once.

And now that the invitation had come, the man who had taken Bert Hensley's place was in charge of deciding whether Michael could accept it or not.

What could be more unfair?

· 3 ·

Grasshoppers flew before the tractor's path, pattering to the ground again like hail. Each sweep of the sickle cut a six-foot swath in the fragrant alfalfa. Michael breathed deeply, filling his lungs with the sweet, green scent.

Dave would let him go. How could he not?

Dave would keep him here. There was no hope.

Why had his mother turned the matter over to Dave, anyway? She had been doing that kind of thing a lot lately, saying, "Ask your father," when he needed permission for anything at all. As though Dave were in charge of him, not her.

Would it help if he agreed to give up the gun, if he told Dave that the .22 rifle wasn't nearly as important as this? Would it help if he got off the tractor and ran back to the barn where Dave was repairing one of the milking machines and said that the only thing he needed, the only thing he *wanted* for his birthday now was a plane ticket to Denver?

It wouldn't even have to be round-trip. If he could just get there, getting back wouldn't be important.

Actually, once he was with his dad, he might never want to come back, anyway.

But then, on the other hand, it would be nice to have both, his new gun and a chance to visit his father, too. He could take the .22 with him when he went to Colorado, and then he and his dad could go hunting again. The last time they had been hunting they had used a single gun between them, but now Michael wasn't "peanut-sized" anymore, so they would need two. That other time they had been hunting, the only time really, they had gotten an enormous, eight-point buck.

It was also the day his father had walked out of the house . . . and never returned.

Michael gazed up at the tree-covered hills as he circled slowly around and around the field. Were these hills he'd grown up with anything like the mountains where his father was? He realized he didn't know. They were substantial hills. The southeastern corner of Minnesota was the only part of the state that hadn't been ground down by the last invasion of glaciers centuries ago. The pictures of mountains in the West that he'd seen hadn't seemed so different from these, but then a picture often didn't give a proper sense of size.

What would he and his dad hunt in the Rocky Mountains? Elk? Deer? Bear, maybe? Michael could see the two of them struggling over a craggy mountainside, following the trail of a wounded bear. An old grizzly they had to gun down before he attacked the town again. It was a dirty job, but somebody had to do it, and they were the ones who had been sent.

A rabbit erupted just before the front wheels of the tractor, and Michael slowed to give the bobbing white tail a clean getaway. It was the one thing he disliked about haying. Sometimes you couldn't avoid hitting small animals or their nests.

He wished he could remember the day he and his dad had been hunting more clearly . . . or without the strange, twisted feeling in his gut that he could never quite explain. As many times as he had gone over the whole thing in his mind, it was always there, the sense that he had done something terribly wrong that day. The sense that it was what he had done that had caused his father to leave.

There were segments that had remained perfectly clear, like the two of them waiting for the buck, somewhere up high, surrounded by leaves. They must have been on a platform in a tree. Afterwards, once he was old enough to be allowed to go into the hills on his own, Michael had tried many times to locate the place. But he had never found even a trace of anything that spoke to him of that day.

He could remember sitting between his father's cocked knees, leaning into the warm wool-and-leather smell. And he, Michael, had been king of the woods, king of all the surrounding farms, king of the deer who were going to come strolling along the trail just below them. He hadn't even minded having to sit very still, to suppress every wiggle, every word.

A deer had arrived, finally, stepping delicately through the fallen leaves, but though his dad raised the rifle, he whispered, his mouth close to Michael's ear, "Not this one. This one's a doe. But just keep watching. I'll bet there'll be a buck with your name on him coming right behind her."

Michael had knelt, peering down the great length of the gun his father held. He had sensed the powerful arms tightening around him and a long, slow intake of breath. And then it had happened. An immense buck moved into the clearing and paused just below them. Paused and waited, as though he knew what he had come for, as though he had, indeed, come bearing Michael's name.

Michael had put his finger on top of his father's on the trigger and sucked in his own breath. Together they squeezed. The gun roared, and the buck, his first and only buck, was down.

After that everything was muddled. He could remember his father's laughter, little more. In fact, occasionally even now, he awakened suddenly in the middle of the night, that same laughter a bright pin in some bursting dream.

It was his father's laughter that ended the firecracker dream sometimes . . . louder even than the explosions of his gun.

The tractor jolted along, rumbling like a large, self-satisfied cat. Michael reached down to untie the old canteen he carried beneath the tractor seat. The water was warm already and tasted of the metal from the canteen. Still the taste was familiar and good. He swished a mouthful and spat it out before taking a long, satisfying drink.

His memory of the hunting didn't end entirely with the death of the buck. He could also remember arriving home with his father after the hunt. At least he remembered the argument his parents had had when they got home. Not their first, by any means. Mostly what he remembered was the ominous hush of voices, quieter than their meaning. The disturbing quiet had followed him even when he had run upstairs and clambered into his bed.

And then his father was gone. He simply went away and never came back. His mother must have known where he was, long enough to get the divorce, anyway, but Michael hadn't seen or heard from him again . . . until today.

His mother had talked to him more than once about kids' feeling responsible when their parents divorced. She had taken great care to explain that a divorce was between two adults, that their kids had nothing to do with it, really. But Michael had always known better. Besides, her very need to explain proved what he already knew. That the argument that final day had been about him. That there really *was* something he had done. Something real bad.

Sometimes he had tried with all his might to remember, figuring that if he only knew he could go back and change it somehow. Or tell somebody he was sorry, at

least. Other times he knew that he couldn't bear to rec-
ollect even the smallest part, that no one, no one on
earth, could live knowing anything so terrible.

It didn't much matter which he wanted, though,
because he had never been able to bring back any of it
except for what he had always known. That he and his
father had gone hunting, that they had gotten their
first buck, and that then his father had left.

Michael finished the last strip of alfalfa, the final
rectangle down the center of the field, and lifting the
sickle, he turned the tractor toward the barn.

All he really needed was a chance to show his dad
how much he had changed. They would go hunting.
And rafting, too. There must be lots of chances for a
person to prove himself whitewater rafting. Whatever
they did, everything would be different this time. *He*
would be different.

Supper was endless. The beef Stroganoff Mom had
made — Michael's favorite — was delicious, as always.
The homemade noodles in their creamy sauce were so
tender they dissolved in the mouth almost without
chewing. The beef could be cut with a fork. But still
Michael ate slowly, his fork hesitating frequently, sus-
pended in the air.

Was Dave never going to decide?

By the time they had finished the German chocolate
cake and then moved to the living room, where Michael
was presented with the single, awkwardly wrapped gift,

he was so heavy with waiting that he hardly cared any longer what he got. Or at least he thought he didn't care until he sat with the rifle across his lap, solid and somehow more real than anything he had ever held before. Certainly more real than the guns he had used in 4-H.

"Thanks, Mom . . . Dave." He could scarcely get out the words.

When he looked up, his mother was smiling, happy in his happiness. Kari sat on the couch between her parents, her gaze intent on the gun. Dave sat with one arm lightly around Kari, his expression serious, almost sad. It was the way he usually looked at Michael these days. He said nothing, though, except, "You know the rules."

Michael nodded. He knew. When he had first begun to talk about wanting a .22, Dave had said, "Sign up for the 4-H Shooting Sports Program first. Then we'll see."

Sometimes he had even quizzed Michael at the table at night about what he was learning. By the time he was done, Michael could have recited gun safety rules in his sleep.

Never keep the gun loaded when he wasn't shooting. Never point at anything he didn't intend to shoot. Always have the safety on, the chamber open, the gun pointed to the ground as he walked. Keep the clip with the ammunition in his pocket until the last minute, just before he was ready to fire. Clean the rifle after every use, keep it rust-free and dry. When the gun wasn't in use, keep it in a place inaccessible to young children, and lock the ammunition away somewhere entirely separate from the gun.

Michael ran his hands over the smoothly grained wood of the stock, crooked his finger in the curve of the trigger. Wait until Gary and Chris saw this. Wait until his dad saw it, for that matter!

"Can I go outside and shoot some pigeons?" Michael remained bent over the rifle as he spoke. The question was too important to take any chances with. Somehow he thought the top of his head was more apt to elicit a yes than the longing his face was sure to show. "You know how you hate the mess they make around the barn."

There was a long silence, and when Michael finally looked up — had to look up, he couldn't stand it any longer — his mother was turned to Dave, waiting as usual for him to answer.

So Michael spoke directly to Dave this time. "I'll be careful. I know all the rules. I'll follow every one, I promise."

"I guess there's no reason for you to have a gun if you aren't allowed to use it," Dave answered at last. "But Michael . . ."

Michael waited.

"No mistakes. With a gun there's no room for mistakes."

He nodded, his heart picking up speed.

"Remember." Dave held his gaze. "Guns kill."

Michael stood, holding the rifle carefully, the muzzle pointed to the floor. "Guns don't kill," he replied cheerfully. "People do." But he saw the moment he had said it that it was the wrong thing.

"People with guns kill a whole lot more often than people without," Dave replied, standing, too.

"Are you going out with him, Dave?" Mom asked, her forehead crumpled, her dark eyes searching Dave's face.

Dave shook his head. "No, Ruth. I don't have the stomach for it."

Kari leaned against their mother, one finger twisting in her pale curls.

"But . . . " Mom was still looking up at Dave. "Do you think it's all right? The first time?"

"He'll be careful," Dave replied, though it didn't sound like a vote of confidence exactly. More like a warning.

"I will," Michael said, and he picked up the box of cartridges that had come with the gun and headed toward the door before his mother could come up with another objection.

"Michael." Dave's voice was abrupt.

Michael stopped in the doorway. He waited without turning back.

"If you kill any birds, bury them out behind the barn. Don't leave them to rot . . . or for me to deal with."

"Yes, sir." Michael glanced over his shoulder. He wanted suddenly to ask, *Have you decided yet? Can I go?* But one look at Dave's face and he knew the decision hadn't been made yet.

He pushed through the screen door and stepped out onto the front porch, cradling his gun in his arms. One thing at a time.

Dave had given in about the rifle. He would do the same about Michael's going to his father.

He had to.

· 4 ·

Nipper emerged from his favorite resting place, a hole he had dug beneath the front porch, and fell into step beside Michael as he moved toward the outbuildings.

"Want to retrieve some birds for me, boy?" Michael asked, rubbing his knuckles on the big dog's bony skull.

Nipper grinned his reply, bouncing heavily a couple of times on stiff front legs, and then moved in close to Michael's side. Michael reached down and pulled the silken warmth of an ear through his fingers as they walked.

One of the barn cats, a long-haired white named Snowball, came to greet them, twining back and forth between Michael's feet. He picked her up and carried her a few steps, but then set her down again. Her fur stood in sticky whorls, thanks to her insistence on letting the new calves nuzzle and suck on her, and Michael wiped his hands on his jeans. He sometimes let the calves suck his own fingers, just to feel their warm, insistent tugging, but there was something distinctly unpleasant about secondhand spit.

For a moment he considered keeping right on going,

walking into the hills and finding himself a buck. But he knew better than that. He didn't have a hunting license, and deer season didn't begin until fall, anyway. Besides, he had told his mom and Dave he was going to shoot pigeons, so it was pigeons he would shoot. He couldn't afford any mistakes now.

On the other side of the barn, he paused by a shed that had been a chicken coop once and was now used for storing machines and various odds and ends. "Sit," he commanded Nipper, and Nipper sat, his floppy ears alert, his head cocked to one side in a mute question.

The pigeons were in their usual location, muttering and cooing among themselves on the top of the machine shed. Without stopping to load the rifle, Michael raised it and focused on the first bird that came into view, a slate gray one silhouetted against the paling sky. The gun's telescopic sight made the bird's form leap toward him.

He lowered the .22 again. Maybe it would be better to start on something else, something closer at hand. He looked around for a target he could set up. Cans. Cans on fence posts. Trash was stored in the shed, so it was a simple matter to find four cans to set up on successive fence posts. This was a safe spot for target practice, too. There was nothing behind the fence except a young cornfield, and a wooded hill behind that would keep bullets from traveling too far.

Michael loaded the clip and snapped it into place, worked the bolt to ready the first cartridge for firing, and raised the gun again. He settled the butt against his shoulder, lifting his right elbow to fit the butt plate into the collarbone pocket as he had been taught at 4-H. His left arm, tight against his side, supported the rifle. He laid his cheek against the cool wood and sighted on a Campbell's soup can, chicken noodle, then clicked the safety off. He was facing Darth Vader. He was about to be attacked by orcs.

"Stand back, Nipper," he said.

POW! The red-and-white can leapt into the air, and the gun's report rattled briefly back and forth between the hills. Nipper whimpered and pulled his head into his shoulders, accordion pleating his loose skin as if trying to disappear inside it.

"Some hunting dog you are!" Michael scolded in mock disgust.

The old dog lowered his chin almost to the ground and peered up at Michael, the bottom of his dark chocolate eyes glistening white.

Michael bent over to touch the top of his head. "Oh, go on, boy. Go home. I'll retrieve my own birds."

Needing no further permission, Nipper slunk away toward the house, his tail tucked, and disappeared beneath the porch.

"A cow retriever." Michael shook his head affectionately. "That's all he's good for." He worked the bolt again, loading another cartridge into the chamber, then paused to admire the rifle. Just wait until Neil Hansen saw it! Wouldn't he be impressed? Maybe even impressed enough to leave Michael alone.

More to the point, wait until his father saw it!

He raised the .22 once more, sighted on the second can, flipped the safety, and fired. This time he missed. There was no evidence of the bullet's passage except the echo ringing back from the hills.

However, the next shot sent the can careening, and the next nicked the third one, tipping it off the fence post in slow motion. One can left. Two more cartridges in the gun. He would make it easily.

"You said you were going to shoot pigeons."

Michael whirled to discover Kari watching him, her arms folded across her chest, her blond curls framing her face like a bright halo.

"I am. I'm just doing a little target practice first, getting the feel of it."

Kari nodded and settled in to watch. Michael wondered, briefly, if she had been given permission to join him. He suspected not. Mom wouldn't have wanted her anywhere near the gun. He rather liked the idea of having her there watching, though, and since nothing had been said to him about keeping her away, he wasn't obligated to send her back.

"I'll show you something." He sighted on the last can and then paused to check over his shoulder to make sure Kari was watching. She was, her round eyes unblinking.

He blasted the can on the first shot and puffed up a spray of dirt right next to where it had fallen on a rapidly fired second.

"Pretty good, huh?"

"Yeah," Kari agreed, though she didn't sound as impressed as he had thought she might. "Now kill a pigeon." She had picked up one of the empty shells cast off from the gun and was turning it over in her fingers.

Michael went cold at the flat way she said it. "Kill a pigeon." If she had said *hit* a pigeon or *get* a pigeon he probably wouldn't have thought anything about it.

"Okay," he said, matching her no-nonsense tone. He reloaded the clip and snapped it into place again, then turned back toward the machine shed. The pigeons had scattered with the sound of his first shot, but they had settled again, apparently deciding, foolishly, that the noise he was making represented no threat.

He raised the rifle once more, sighting first on one bird, then on another. He settled on a lavender one with purplish wings. The telescopic sight brought the pale breast close. If he concentrated hard enough, he could almost see the soft feathers rise and fall with the pigeon's breath.

He lowered the gun and looked back at Kari again. "Are you sure you want to watch?"

"Uh-huh," she replied.

"When I shoot it, it'll be dead. Do you know what that means?"

Her eyes were almost the lavender of the pigeon's breast, and they didn't waver from his face. "Yeah," she said. "I know."

"Okay," he told her gruffly. "Okay. You asked for it."

He raised the gun once more, sighted, picked out the light-breasted bird again, and then moved from it to the one he had drawn his sights on at first, the one that was slate gray all over. His palms were beginning to sweat.

Once more he lowered the gun. "Maybe you'd better go back up to the house, Kari. I'll bet Mom doesn't want you here. Nipper already went back, you know."

"Nipper's scared of loud noises," she answered. "I'm not."

"You're scared of blood, though. Aren't you?"

She shook her head emphatically, whipping her delicate curls back and forth with the movement.

Again Michael turned toward the machine shed. He cocked the .22 and raised it to his shoulder.

The pigeons had been hopping over one another, settling and resettling on the peak of the roof, and neither the pale one nor the slate gray afforded a good shot any longer. The gun wavered with the pull of its own weight while Michael tried to make another choice. The birds appeared and disappeared in the telescopic sight as if they were the ones moving, not the gun.

"Just a minute," he said finally. "I've got to get something to steady my gun. It's pretty heavy."

He checked the safety and laid the rifle on the ground. Then he looked around. To one side of the shed was an old sawhorse. He dragged it over to his spot, knelt, and took up the rifle again, propping the barrel on the crossbar of the sawhorse this time.

He could feel Kari's gaze like a pressure against his skin. But now he could pick out a pigeon with ease. The slate gray was in range again. It stood out against the first faint coloring of the western sky like a dark sentinel. Michael moved the gun and sighted another bird, this one almost sky colored. Maybe it was the lavender one again. The quality of the light was changing, and he couldn't tell for sure. This bird was turning, raising its wings. Yes, the wings were deep purple, the exact shade of the hills after the sun had gone down.

"Aren't you going to shoot?"

The sound of Kari's voice made Michael jerk. "Hush," he ordered. "I have to concentrate."

When he had focused again, the sky-colored pigeon was gone. *See*, he wanted to say to Kari, *see, it's your fault*. But he didn't say it. He knew it wouldn't make any sense.

He moved the gun slowly, searching for another good shot. The slate gray came into view once more. In the magnification of the scope, Michael could see the pigeon's head turning until a single, dark eye seemed to be looking back at him. His hands tightened on the .22.

Not this one. He didn't know why, but he rather liked this dark bird, which seemed to stand out from the rest. Besides, it made him feel a bit like God, deciding who would live and who would die. He pivoted the rifle to try for another shot.

"If you don't want to, can I?"

Michael stopped, closed his eyes for a few seconds and then got to his feet slowly to face his sister. "If I don't want to what?"

"If you don't want to shoot a pigeon."

"You think it's so easy, shooting pigeons? You think it's something any little five-year-old can do?"

Kari didn't bother to answer that. She seemed to be waiting, still, for an answer to her own question.

Anger swept through Michael like fire through dry grass, though he couldn't have said what it was exactly that he was angry about. "If you think it's so easy, you go ahead," he challenged, holding the rifle out to Kari. "Shoot one."

Kari reached for the gun, her face lighting up.

Startled at her eagerness, Michael almost withdrew the gun. If his parents found out he had let her shoot his rifle, he would get into trouble for sure. But then, how would they find out? Kari wouldn't be the one to run and tell them. She wasn't like other little kids that way. And with all the drilling Dave had done about rules of safety, no one had said a word about not letting Kari shoot his gun. Besides, Michael's dad had let him shoot when he was exactly Kari's age, hadn't he?

"Come on," he said gruffly. "I'll show you how."

The rifle was almost as tall as Kari, but she took it firmly, resting the butt on the ground.

Michael set her up in front of the sawhorse, the rifle's barrel propped on the crossbar, and began to explain.

"That's the scope. Look through it. Whatever you want to shoot needs to be right where those two hairs cross in the middle."

"Can I shoot a pigeon?" she asked, squinting to see through the scope.

Michael laughed. "Sure. If you can hit one. It's not easy. They aren't very big, and they're pretty far away."

The gun wavered as Kari pointed it toward the top of the shed. Michael reached around her to steady it, holding the rifle loosely so she could still aim.

"Can you see?" he asked. "Tell me when you're ready."

"No," she said, and then, excitement coloring her voice, "Yes! I can. I can see a pigeon."

"Are you ready to shoot?"

"Yes." The word was breathed more than it was spoken.

Michael reached forward to take the safety off. "Fire when ready."

Almost instantly the gun let out a sharp report, and Kari jerked at the sound of her own shot. Michael steadied her as well as the gun. She felt so small inside the circle of his arms. Could he possibly have felt as small when his father had held him?

A dozen pigeons, two dozen, rose from the machine shed in a tumult of fluttering wings. As far as Michael could see, nothing more had happened. The pigeons had flown in response to the noise as they had when he was shooting at the cans.

"I got one," Kari announced with that absolute confidence of hers, ducking to escape Michael's confinement and leaving the gun with him.

"Oh, I don't think so." Michael put the safety on again. "I told you it was going to be pretty hard."

"But I did. I got one. I saw." Kari had turned to confront him, her jaw set, small fists cocked on her hips.

Michael smiled at her certainty. Sometimes he wished he could be as sure about everything as she was. "Go see if you can find it, then." He began polishing the barrel of the .22 on the front of his shirt.

Kari took off at a run, disappearing around the back of the shed . . . and returned almost immediately. She was holding the limp form of a pigeon. The slate gray one. The one Michael had decided not to shoot.

The pigeon's head lolled from its body at an acute angle, though the one dark eye Michael could see still seemed to be alert and staring. The evening light caught the neck feathers, giving them an iridescence he hadn't been able to detect when he had been studying the bird earlier through the scope of the rifle.

The feathers weren't just gray. They were purple, pink, blue . . . even green. Infinitely various. A spot of dark blood, too dark to be called red, oozed from the bird's breast.

"See!" Kari was triumphant. "I told you."

Michael laid down the .22, carefully, slowly, and took the pigeon, still warm and somehow boneless. He looked from Kari to the blood oozing onto the multicolored feathers. A few drops puddled in his hand. His father's hands had been bloody, too, after he had started to clean the buck. His father's hands had dripped blood, and still he had laughed.

But Michael looked down at the warm color gathering in his palm, and something deep inside him turned over.

"See what you've done!" He held the dead bird toward Kari, thrust it at her so she would have to look. "See? Maybe this bird had babies somewhere. Did you think about that? And now they'll starve, because no one will come to feed them!"

Kari's mouth dropped, and she began to back away, tears springing to her eyes. "I . . . I . . . didn't mean," she stammered.

"Of course you meant." He was shouting now. "Kill a pigeon. That's what you said. You wanted to kill a pigeon!" He followed Kari's retreat, shifting the feathery corpse to his other hand and holding his bloody palm up to her face.

"No, Michael!"

But Michael wouldn't be stopped, couldn't have stopped himself if he had wanted to. "You did it," he cried. "You killed it! You!"

When she tried to duck, to get away from him, he grabbed for her. His hand brushed across her face, leaving a glistening red streak the length of one cheek. She gasped, stood perfectly still, one small hand raised to touch the dampness.

"Michael!" Their mother appeared around the edge of the barn. "Did Kari come out here with — "

Michael turned to face his mother, still clutching the dead bird in one hand, wiping the other on his jeans. But before he could speak, before he could begin to explain, he saw her go pale. Her hands sprang to her mouth.

"Oh, my God," she cried. "Oh, my God!"

And Kari was stumbling toward her, tears running down her face and mingling with the pigeon's blood.

· 5 ·

I don't understand." Dave sat on the living room couch with the .22 across his lap, his huge hands wrapped around it in a way that made the gun appear to be already locked away. "Why would you attack your sister like that?"

Michael sat slumped over, studying the floor between his feet. It was one of those questions for which there was clearly no answer. At least none that was going to help. "I guess she made me mad," he said miserably.

"You guess she made you mad," Dave repeated in an uninflected voice. "And so you rubbed blood on her face?"

Michael shrugged. He hadn't meant to do that. At least he didn't think he had. And he could hardly explain that Kari had shot *his* pigeon, the one he had decided to let live. He didn't understand, himself, why that should have made him so angry.

The only good thing about the whole mess was that neither Dave nor his mother had figured out that Kari had been using his gun. In all the commotion following Mom's arrival, Kari hadn't once revealed that. Michael wasn't sure whether she had been protecting him or herself. Both, probably. She would have gotten into trouble, too, if their parents had known. Nonetheless, Michael was grateful for her silence.

Not that things could have been much worse for him. Dave was going to take the gun away, he was certain of that. The only thing that remained to be seen was for how long. A week? A month?

Michael looked down at his hands. The blood on them had dried to the color of ordinary dirt. He rubbed at it with his thumb, flaking it away.

Kari was such a little kid. She probably didn't understand yet about things dying, about death being so . . . permanent.

Michael thought of the still body of the pigeon left lying out by the shed where he had dropped it after his mother had gone back to the house with Kari. He would have to remember to bury it. Bury the pigeon and pick up the cans he'd used for target practice. Otherwise he would end up being in trouble for that, too.

But then what did it matter, being in more trouble? He had only one gun to lose. Except that now he had probably lost the chance to go to his father also.

He glanced up and immediately down again. Dave was sitting across the room with his hands still enfolding the gun. Like a guard overseeing a convict. Michael could hear bathwater splashing and his mother and Kari talking upstairs. The sound was so normal as to be almost reassuring.

He hadn't meant to do anything bad to Kari. He didn't know what he had meant, really.

Dave broke the silence finally. "I'm going to have to put your gun away," he said. "But then I'm sure you knew that."

"Yes." Michael knew, but still he hated the way Dave said it. *I'm going to have to,* as though that wasn't what he had wanted all along, as though some power he had no control over were forcing him to take Michael's .22.

"Maybe next year . . ."

Michael looked up sharply. Dave couldn't mean it. Not that long! He waited, but the words remained there in the air, unfinished. Unchanged.

"Next year?" he asked finally, holding his voice as steady as he could. "You're going to make me wait a whole year because of one little mistake?"

"Smearing your sister with blood wasn't exactly a little mistake. It's the kind of thing that makes it clear you aren't yet mature enough — "

Michael rose from his chair. Rather, the chair seemed to propel him forward into motion. "You've no right." He heard his own words as though from a great distance, dangerous and low. "None at all."

"I have more than a right, Michael. I have a responsibility."

Michael stood there, halfway across the room, a bubble of rage expanding inside his chest. "No!" He shook his head violently. "Just because you married my mother, just because you went to the courthouse and got a piece of paper, that doesn't make you responsible for me. You're not my father, you know."

He had never said such a thing before. He had never even said it to his mother. *You mustn't feel that way!* she would have said, as if feelings were something that could be turned off and on with musts . . . and must nots.

Dave studied him for a long time, his eyes the bright blue at the center of a flame. "What do you want me to do?" he asked finally.

"Let me go." Michael's heart was thumping, but he spoke calmly. "Just let me go to Colorado. To my father. He invited me. He wants me. I belong there with him."

Dave sighed deeply, and something invisible that usually held his back erect seemed to disengage. His shoulders slumped, and he looked down at the .22 rifle in his lap. After a long silence he said, "Maybe that's the best thing I can do for you." He said it quietly, without looking up.

Michael's joints went soft. He couldn't believe it. He wanted to accept his father's invitation more than he had ever wanted anything in his life, more than he had ever wanted the gun even, but he hadn't really expected Dave to agree. "You mean it? You're going to let me go?"

Dave looked at Michael directly now, and Michael realized he had been wrong about his eyes. They weren't blue flame at all. They were ice. Still, the man nodded, and the nod was all Michael needed.

"I'll tell Mom you decided." Michael spoke quietly,

already easing himself toward the stairs, as if Dave's decision were some kind of spell that might be broken by noise or sudden movement.

On the bottom step, he turned back with one hand on the bannister. "Would you — " He hesitated. *Would you let me take my gun?* was what he was going to say. *My dad and I will want to go hunting*. But he stopped, shook his head to indicate he had changed his mind about what he had started to say.

Dave looked so defeated somehow, sitting there cradling the .22, that Michael couldn't ask. It didn't matter, anyway. His dad would have a gun for him to use. He might even have one to give him . . . a gun nobody in the world, including Dave, would be able to take away.

Michael stood in front of the cracked mirror he kept propped on his bedroom dresser and stared at his reflection. It had been three days since Dave had agreed to let him go to his father, and he was leaving the next day. After waiting more than half his lifetime, he was going at last.

What would his father see when he looked at him? *I'll bet you're a big, strapping fellow now*, he had said. Would he be disappointed?

Michael flexed his biceps. Would Bert Hensley recognize how strong his son was, that he could sling bales of hay, drive a tractor? That he could paddle a raft down a mountain river? Once he learned how, of course.

The plans for the trip were all set now. Michael had

called and left a message for his father, who had called him back. His dad had seemed really happy when Michael had said he could come. Michael didn't tell him that his adoptive father, Dave, whatever the man was to be called, was the one who had given him permission. He didn't add, either, that it wasn't really a visit. That he meant to stay. They would work all that out when he got there.

He would miss his mom. In fact, he'd miss her something fierce. He'd miss the farm, too, and Nipper . . . and his buddies. He would even miss Kari. But he couldn't get over how delighted his father had sounded. Michael didn't know when anyone had ever sounded so pleased about seeing *him*.

He leaned forward until his nose almost touched the glass. It was an old mirror he had rescued from the trash years before. His mother had thrown it out when it had fallen off the wall and cracked. She didn't need it, anyway. She had a full-length mirror on the back of her bedroom door for checking her clothes and another above her dressing table for applying makeup.

He didn't know why it was that women and girls always had mirrors. Even men had small ones to shave by. But no one ever thought of giving a mirror to a boy. As if boys weren't supposed to want to know what they looked like.

Most of the time, it hadn't really been his own image that had interested Michael, though. It was the other world the mirror held, the sense of possibilities he'd never been able to find on this side of the glass.

In the mirror world, there was his bed, looking like a rumpled nest slept in by some stranger. His 4-H trophy and the ribbons, all of them won by his red Guernsey, Rilda. They looked shinier, more brightly colored on the other side. Even the reversed titles of the books on his shelf were mysterious and alluring, as if in that reflected world he might read them all again and find their stories new.

But most inviting of all was the place where the mirror image stopped, the unseen room beyond. When he was younger he had believed, quite literally, that there was something hidden there, just beyond the inspection of his eye. Something that didn't exist at all in the world he knew.

It was where he used to imagine his father had gone and was waiting to be found.

When Michael was told in science class that nothing was solid, that the entire world was composed of moving atoms, he had come home and tried to reach through the mirror with his hand. He had thought that if he closed his eyes so that he wasn't aware of the nonsolid atoms of his hand coming into contact with those of the mirror, he could find his way into that other world . . . like Alice.

He didn't care for the Alice stories, really. Never had. Reading them was like being caught in someone else's nightmare. And he was too much of a farm boy to be fascinated by rabbit holes. Rabbit holes held rabbits. Nothing more.

But mirrors. Mirrors were something else entirely.

Would he have a mirror in his father's house? he wondered. It didn't matter. Once he was with his father, there would be nothing more to look for.

His bedroom door swung open behind him, and Michael watched the reflected movement without turning. It was Kari. She was wearing a long, flower-sprigged nightgown that made her look like a Christmas-card cherub.

As usual, she came straight to the point. "You're going away," she said, her lower lip thrust out in a most uncherublike pout.

"Yeah." Michael spoke to the Kari in the mirror. "I am. I'm going to see my father. My *real* father," he added, wondering if she understood the concept. Had anyone ever explained to her about his other, real father?

"Why are you — "

"Because he invited me. Because it's where I belong."

"No," she shook her head emphatically, impatient with his interruption. "Why are you looking at the mirror?"

Michael shrugged. How did you answer a kid like that? "I'm not looking at the mirror. I'm looking at my room, you, everything here. So I can remember it while I'm gone."

Kari nodded, as though his answer made perfect sense, but apparently there was another question she had come to ask, because she remained standing there.

Michael waited, studying her reflection. Her face was

set in a thoughtful frown that showed clearly she was working something out.

"Are you my brother?" she asked finally.

"Your half brother," he answered. "I have a different father than you do."

She shook her head again. "No, you're not."

"I'm not what?"

"Half my brother."

Michael restrained a smile. He remembered how he had hated to be laughed at when he was a little kid. "Why do you say that?"

"Because you're the only one I got," she replied, with indisputable logic, and then she disappeared.

Michael gazed at the reflection of the empty doorway and the shadowed hall.

He hadn't told Kari the truth. He realized that immediately. He wasn't remembering things here, memorizing them to carry away like a picture in a frame the way he had said. He was getting ready to pass through to the other side.

He took a step closer, and the diagonal crack in the glass separated his face into two sections, each side slightly out of kilter with the other. Like two puzzle pieces that didn't fit. One half running off after his father, one staying here with his mother and Dave on the farm.

But then he moved again, and he was whole once more, whole and on his way. His father was waiting.

· 6 ·

Michael's mother reached into her purse and came up with the envelope that contained his plane ticket. "Here it is," she said, but then she sat holding it instead of handing it to him.

Somewhere along the corridor of the airport a voice was bellowing through a loudspeaker, but Michael could barely make out the words. Something about Chicago, a flight to Chicago. It wasn't his.

He resisted the impulse to snatch the ticket out of his mother's hand. Instead, he stood to check on Kari. She had wandered over to the window in the waiting area to watch the planes. Now she was standing with her nose pressed against the heavy glass, as though that last quarter inch made all the difference.

Michael sat down again. He was tempted to join Kari, but it was such a little-kid activity. Besides, he might as well stay and listen to more instructions. If he didn't hear them all now, Mom might follow him up the ramp, still talking.

Just because he had never flown before, his mother seemed to think he needed to have every single thing explained. She had even asked if she should tell an attendant to stay with him in Denver until he was met. At least she had *asked*, not just gone ahead and done it. Imagine how embarrassing it would have been to be handed over to his father by some flight attendant as though he were still five years old!

"Michael, this ticket . . ."

He flinched. He hoped she wasn't going to tell him to remind his father about repaying the cost of the flight. She had wanted his dad to buy the tickets in Colorado and mail them. There was no travel agency near Salida, though, so Dad had asked her to pay for them instead. He had said he would reimburse her. Mom had made a comment about that, something under her breath that Michael hadn't quite caught, hadn't wanted to catch.

"I paid full price," she continued, "because that way you can exchange your return ticket and come back any time you like . . . in case you decide a month is too long."

"Or not long enough," Michael added, instantly irritated. What did she think, that his father was some stranger whom he might discover he didn't like? That after being kept from him all these years he would even consider coming home early?

"No." Her voice was firm. "We agreed to a month. No more. Your being gone will be hard enough on Dave as it is."

And we wouldn't want anything to be hard on Dave, would we? But Michael didn't say that.

She added, more softly, "And me. It'll be hard on me, too."

He nodded. He knew that. It would be hard on her in a whole different way. Dave would miss the extra pair of hands at the chores. She would miss *him*.

Maybe she was afraid of losing him. Maybe she should have thought of that before she'd divorced his father.

Not that he wouldn't miss her, too. He would. His mom and the farm, too. It hardly seemed possible to separate the two of them in his mind. As hard as to separate himself from either.

But then the voice was blaring again, close at hand now, and this time it was his flight. Michael stood, reaching for the ticket still in his mother's hand. His stomach seemed to be screwed into his backbone, and too tightly. Mom stood, too, but instead of giving him the ticket, she opened her arms and drew him into a fierce hug. He hugged her back, equally hard. Who knew when he would see her again . . . or Kari?

"Thanks, Mom. Thanks for letting me go."

"It's Dave who gave you permission," she reminded him, always the advocate for Dave. She had stepped back to study his face.

"Yeah. Dave gave me permission, but you're the one who's letting me go."

She smiled at that, but the smile passed quickly and she went back to looking worried, the way she had been all week. "Just . . . oh, Michael" — she pulled him to her again — "just be careful. Okay?"

"Sure, Mom. Don't worry. I'll be fine." He patted her back, exactly the way he soothed Kari when she was frightened or hurt. "Besides, I'm not going to be on my own, you know. My dad will be there."

"Yes, of course." She released him finally and tried to toss off a small laugh. "I'm being foolish, I know."

The man with the microphone was talking again. Did he say those in row twenty-seven and higher should board the plane now? Michael was in row thirty-two. He held out his hand, and his mother relinquished the ticket, finally.

"Kari," he called, "I'm going now." But Kari continued to gaze stubbornly out the window. She was angry with Michael for leaving and had been that way the whole morning.

"I'm sorry Dave couldn't come to see you off," Mom said as Michael shouldered his knapsack. It contained a couple of books, some homemade oatmeal cookies she had insisted on sending along, and several odds and ends that wouldn't fit into his suitcase. "But you know how it is. When the ladies — "

"Have to be milked, they have to be milked," Michael finished for her, and then they both laughed. It was an old, old joke.

Michael kissed her, a quick peck on the cheek. He thought of calling to Kari again, but then he decided to let it go. To let *her* go with her silly pouting. He stepped into the line moving steadily toward the ramp door and gave his mother a final wave. Then he turned away and didn't look back again. She could stand there, if she must, looking faintly injured as though someone were stealing something that belonged exclusively to her.

He was going to Colorado . . . to his father.

I'm coming, Dad, he called in the inward way he and his father had spoken for years. *I'm on my way.*

And his father called back, his voice joyous and strong, *Come along, Mike. I'm here!*

As soon as Michael stepped inside the door to the waiting area at the Denver airport, he separated himself from the stream of disembarking passengers and looked around eagerly. Would Dad recognize him? Maybe it would be up to him to recognize his father. Adults didn't change so much in eight years.

He knew exactly what his father looked like. Brown hair like his own, slightly wavy. Slender, but tall, strong. And his eyes were . . . What were they? Blue? Brown?

It didn't matter. You didn't need to know the color of a person's eyes to recognize him in an airport.

There were a lot of people milling around. Michael set his knapsack down and squared his shoulders. There was a man in a cowboy hat and boots who seemed to be looking for someone. His protruding belly flaunted a massive silver-and-turquoise belt buckle. He was coming toward Michael. Surely not . . .

The cowboy threw his arms around a woman emerging from the ramp just behind Michael. Michael couldn't help letting out a sigh of relief. He had known the man wasn't his father, of course. Still, after all this time it was hard to be sure of anything. He picked up his knapsack and moved deeper into the room.

Maybe Dad had been delayed. He had said it was a

three-and-a-half-hour drive from Salida to the Denver airport. "I'll be there unless we have snow," he had explained. "Sometimes the passes get closed then."

Michael had laughed at the idea of snow in June, but his father had been serious. Apparently summer was never a certainty in the mountains.

Michael set his knapsack down again and shoved his hands into his pockets. He adjusted his shoulders to what felt like a jaunty angle. He certainly didn't want to be looking like a scared kid when Dad found him. How was it that adults always managed to seem so casual, so on top of it all, as though they already had everything in the world figured out and no place was ever new or strange?

"Hello. Are you Mike Hensley . . . I mean Ostrom?"

Michael jumped. The person who had spoken to him was definitely not his father. In fact, it — she — was a woman. And more woman than Michael had ever seen in a single package before.

She must have been six feet tall, at least. And everything about her was larger than life. Not fat, certainly, just . . . abundant. Even her hair seemed too full, too rich to be mere hair. It was a dark red-gold that lapped around her shoulders and down her back like tongues of flame. And her eyes were, incredibly, the same color as her hair. Too warm, too alive, too filled with light to be called brown.

"Mike?" the giantess repeated.

Michael nodded, unable to speak.

"I'm Cil." She held out a hand.

Michael stared at it. It was as though his tongue was paralyzed, his hands lashed to his sides.

"Short for Priscilla," she added, wrinkling her nose exactly the way Kari did over something that she found objectionable. "Anyway," Cil continued, with a tone of apology, as though her name — or his inability to speak or move — were all her fault, "Cil's much better than Prissy."

"Yes, of course it is," Michael said, finding his tongue at last and saying, he realized the instant he had opened his mouth, the wrong thing. He should have told this woman he liked the name Priscilla. That Prissy was just fine, too, for that matter. And then, blushing, he stuck out his hand, too late, because she had finally dropped hers, and added, "I'm Michael. I mean, Mike."

She put her hand out again, too, but by that time Michael's was no longer there. He was wiping the damp from his palm onto his shirt. Cil looked down at her empty hand, at his fumbling, threw back her head, and laughed, a kind of musical roar.

Michael felt himself flush. Was she laughing at him? No. It didn't feel that way. More *with* him, whenever he might choose to join her, and he managed to push out a couple of small giggles.

"Where's my dad?" he asked when Cil picked up his knapsack and started out of the waiting area. "Is he outside?"

"He told me to tell you he was real sorry, Mike . . ." She was reading overhead signs directing them through the airport as she moved, and her voice trailed off.

At the words *real sorry* Michael's heart lurched. His father had changed his mind. He didn't want Michael here, after all! Cil had been sent to tell him he was to return to Minnesota on the next plane. But then, as quickly as the despair had come it lifted. Why hadn't he thought of it? Snow!

"The pass must be closed, huh?" he inquired.

Cil stopped walking and looked down at him, her expression confused. "The pass closed?"

"With snow. Dad said he'd be here to meet me unless it snowed and they closed the pass."

A smile tweaked at the corners of her mouth, but she said only, "Not in June. Besides, I came through it myself this morning. I work for River Rafters, too."

"It could have been snowed in, though," Michael argued. Why did he feel as though his father's honor was under attack?

"It's possible, I suppose," Cil replied agreeably. Then she shook her head. "Your dad's always looking for excitement of some kind, even if he has to manufacture June blizzards." She said it with affection, though.

"Then what's wrong? Where is he?" Michael asked the question though he wasn't sure he wanted to hear the answer.

"Oh, nothing's wrong. He just had to work, that's all. At the last minute we had some mers wanting to do the Royal Gorge, and he was the only boatman not already assigned who's qualified for that stretch."

"*Mers?*" Michael inquired. Cil had begun moving again, so he kept pace beside her, though it took nearly two of his steps to equal one of hers.

"Customers. I guess we get to talking our own language on the river. Mers . . . customers. Peeps . . . people. Wannabees are the ones who watch but are too scared to try the river themselves."

"Oh." Michael struggled between disappointment and resignation. He'd been waiting for eight years, and his father couldn't come to get him. Because he had to work. But then a person couldn't help having to work. Even Michael had to go home for chores sometimes when he'd rather be doing something else.

Following the signs that said To Baggage Claim, Cil stepped onto a moving walkway, and Michael followed. He wanted to take his knapsack from her. It wasn't right, this woman carrying his stuff as though he couldn't have managed it himself. The idea of grabbing it away seemed more rude than letting her carry it, however, so he did nothing.

"What's the Royal Gorge?" he asked instead.

She turned back to answer. "It's seven miles of the most intense white water in Colorado. Almost constant rapids. Most of them rated four or five." Michael must have looked blank, because Cil added, "A rating of six means a rapid is unrunnable."

"Oh," Michael said again, and he could have kicked himself. Some conversationalist he was turning out to be. He was nearly as bad as Dave.

But he wasn't going to think about Dave. He was

here, in Colorado, with his father. Or he would be with him very soon. He tried to think of something else to say, something that would keep Cil talking to him.

"Do you work in the office?" he asked.

Cil looked blank.

"At the River Rafters, I mean. Are you the secretary?" The two times he had called to leave messages for his father he had spoken to a woman in the River Rafters' office. Maybe it had been Cil.

Cil scowled and tossed her head so the mass of fiery hair tumbled about. "So . . ." she said, "you're a bit of a male chauvinist, are you?"

Michael ducked his head. Once more he could feel the heat climbing his neck to his face. He wasn't sure what she meant. He knew what a male chauvinist was . . . more or less. But he didn't know how he had suddenly come to be one.

Cil put a warm hand on his shoulder. If his question had offended her, she was over the offense almost instantly. "I'm a boatman," she explained, "a guide. Like your father. Only I'm not qualified to run the Royal Gorge with paying passengers yet. I will be before the summer is over, though."

Would he ever quit saying the wrong thing? Michael covered his embarrassment by nodding vigorously to show Cil how certain he was she would qualify for the Royal Gorge very soon. Now that he thought about it, she looked strong enough to run just about anything she might choose. Niagara Falls, maybe.

"Do you want to go with me on my qualifying run?" Cil asked, a teasing twinkle in her golden eyes.

"Sure." He nodded more vigorously still.

She studied his face for a moment before asking, quite solemnly, "You're not afraid of dying?"

A conversation with this woman made Michael feel that he already knew what running the Royal Gorge would be like. But his answer came popping out of its own accord, quite unplanned, even unanticipated. "Naw." He chuckled to show Cil how easy he was. "Not if I get to die with you."

Cil threw back her head and laughed, and the laugh prompted Michael to join her this time, heartily.

"A chip off the old block," she said, and though Michael wasn't entirely sure why she had said that either, he laughed some more.

· 7 ·

"Here we are," Cil said, pulling off the road and bumping through the scrub brush. She brought her Volkswagen beetle to a stop behind a battered green pickup.

Here we are? Michael looked around. There was no house. Only an old trailer — not even a house trailer but the kind people used for camping — set down in the midst of a plot of empty land. To one side of the trailer, almost hidden in some scrubby trees, there was a small, tar paper–covered structure, obviously an out-house. Did his father live without plumbing . . . in a camping trailer?

They had left the town of Salida behind by several miles, and snowcapped mountains rose on each side of the valley, range after range. Each range looked mistier, less real than the one before. The smallest of the mountains would have dwarfed the hills Michael knew at home. And made entirely of jagged stone, they were far more forbidding than the hills. Even in the bottom of the valley the land was more like rocky desert than the verdant summer growth he was accustomed to.

Michael squared his shoulders as he climbed out of

the car. It wasn't what he had expected, but if this was where his dad lived, it was where he wanted to be, too. No complaints.

A man — it had to be his father — burst from the trailer and started toward them at a loping stride. He was smaller than Michael had remembered, both shorter and slighter. In fact, Michael could see as he approached that his dad was a good four or five inches shorter than Cil. His hair was dark and slightly wavy, though, exactly as Michael had remembered.

"Well," he was saying, even as he approached. "Well." And he came to a halt in front of Michael, his face radiant. "Here you are! At last!" He took Michael's hand . . . just grabbed it up and enclosed it in the warm cup created by both of his. His palms were calloused, his clasp strong. And then, apparently finding that action insufficient, he dropped the hand and seized Michael instead. He swung him around so that his feet left the ground, and he laughed, a laugh filled with delight. Cil had to step back to keep from getting kicked.

He talked even as they spun around, the words tumbling out in a jerky stream. "Mike! It's been so long. So long. It's good to see you. I hardly knew what to expect. We've got to get to know one another all over again, don't we? You and me." He staggered to a stop and set Michael on his feet, then stood back and looked him up and down. "God, Cil, isn't he a good-looking kid?"

Released, Michael tottered to catch his balance.

Cil nodded, beaming approval as though she were

responsible for producing Michael, not merely for delivering him to his father's door.

Michael could feel the dizzy smile that covered his face, but he couldn't seem to find anything to say. His tongue formed a speechless knot that occupied his entire mouth as it had at the airport with Cil.

His father, however, went on talking, apparently not noticing. Or perhaps he noticed and understood. Maybe he was just giving Michael time. "Steak," he was saying. "I got us each a thick steak for tonight. To hell with the cost. My son is back."

Michael was surprised when his father said that, *My son is back*, as though Michael had been the one to go away, not he. Michael didn't care, though. He did feel, curiously, as if he were returning home.

"This is some kid you've got, Bert," Cil said.

"He sure is," his dad said, more calmly now, more matter-of-factly. And then, apparently in continuation of some earlier discussion, "Didn't I tell you, Cil?"

She nodded, agreeing that he had.

Michael could have exploded with pure pleasure, but there were no words for his joy. He simply stood there, his cheeks still stretched into what must have been a foolish grin.

Dad finally nudged him into action. "Where's your stuff? In the car? Get it and I'll show you where you'll be bunking."

Michael trotted to Cil's car and returned, lugging his large suitcase, his knapsack slung over his shoulder. He could feel his father watching him the whole time. In fact, now that the first greeting had cooled, he was examining Michael with the kind of appraising look a man might use who was about to make a bid on a piece of livestock.

"With all that milk and cheese, I thought they grew them big in Minnesota," he said, as Michael let the heavy suitcase drop to the ground. Then he laughed, as though that could erase the sting of the words.

Cil scolded the man in a good-natured way. "Come on, Bert, give him a chance. The kid stands tall in my book."

Michael's face burned. He didn't know where to look. No place felt quite safe. Why had his father said that, about his being small? He wasn't so darned big himself! Why had Cil jumped to defend him, just like his mother with Dave?

He and Cil had gotten to know one another pretty well during the long drive to Salida. He had found out that she had been a junior high English teacher until last season, when she had quit teaching to follow the rafting season through the full year. Now she went to West Virginia in the fall and then on to New Zealand for the winter so she could work as a guide all year long. Michael had tried to imagine having an English teacher like Cil, but the idea was beyond imagining.

His father bowed to Cil's mild reprimand. "Certainly, he stands tall," he agreed. "Certainly!" And he touched the top of Michael's head as though taking and approving his measure.

Michael wasn't sure how he felt about this sudden

turn and turnabout, so he chose to feel nothing. As his father had said, they had to get to know one another again. There were bound to be some awkward moments in the beginning.

He picked up his things, and he and his father moved toward the trailer, Cil following. The heavy suitcase banged clumsily against his leg, but Dad didn't offer to help. Michael was glad. Cil had relinquished his knapsack at the airport only to carry the heavier suitcase. It hadn't even seemed to occur to her that he might have preferred to manage both himself.

Dad was saying, "You can unpack, and I'll get the steaks going. You must be starved. The stuff they feed you on an airplane would hardly make a dent in a growing boy like you."

He opened the door and ushered Michael into the trailer.

Cil waited outside as if she figured she was too big to fit inside with the two of them. And it was, indeed, a very small trailer. A tiny gas stove, a sink, and a cooler occupied one wall. A couch took up the other. Just beyond the couch, at one end, there was a small table and two built-in benches. With enough room for two to sit, no more. At the other end a curtain was pushed aside, revealing a bed.

"This'll be yours, Mike," his father said, indicating the couch. "And this is where you can put your things." He reached down and pulled out a single drawer from beneath the couch.

"Thanks," Michael said. It was, he realized, the first word he had uttered since arriving.

His father nodded pleasantly. "Now . . . Cil and I'll get the steaks on, and you come out as soon as you're ready. Okay?"

And the next thing Michael knew, he was standing alone, looking from his suitcase and knapsack to the drawer his father had assigned him. It was, he knew, going to be much too small to hold what he had brought.

Still, he began to unpack.

· 8 ·

Michael stuffed the last of what he could make fit into the drawer and jammed it closed. He set his knapsack, which was still full, on the floor next to the couch and shoved the only partially empty suitcase to one side. Then he sat down and looked around. So this was his father's place. His place, too, now.

It didn't look like much.

Was his father poor? Michael had never conceived of such a possibility. His family wasn't wealthy by any means — there were times when money was pretty tight — but they lived entirely differently than this. You would think whitewater guides would be paid well, if only for the danger they faced every day, but that didn't seem to be the case.

The trailer showed numerous signs of age and hard use, though it was neat and clean, everything in its place. *Shipshape* was the word that came to mind. The walls were papered in a hunting motif, and the paper was the only thing that looked as though it might have been a recent addition. It was the kind of wallpaper he would have expected his father to choose, the kind he would have chosen, too.

The repeated picture was of long grass at the edge of water, two bird dogs standing at point, ducks silhouetted against a rising (or was it setting?) sun. The hunters weren't visible, but you knew they were there, just behind the tallest clump of grass.

On the wall above the couch hung a .22 rifle, a semiautomatic. Michael turned from his examination of the paper to run his fingers along the sleek barrel. He would have to talk to his dad about going hunting. Too bad he hadn't been able to bring his own gun.

He leaned back, narrowing his eyes and focusing on the lead duck in the wallpaper scene. There were certain kinds of pictures that had always had a special power over Michael, pictures that pulled him inside like magnets. They could be hanging on a wall or in a book or even part of wallpaper, like these. They were always small scenes into which he could project himself, imagine himself walking a cobbled street or penetrating a wilderness forest . . . or watching the flight of ducks with his gun at the ready.

He turned again to touch his father's rifle. He wanted to hold it. Nothing more. He wanted, just for a moment, to be part of the wallpaper scene, to imagine himself at his dad's side. He knew that no duck hunter would be using a .22, but such details weren't important. He wasn't going to fire the rifle anyway. He knelt on the couch.

The gun came off the pegs and settled into his hands as though it had been waiting all this time for his arrival.

"You unpacked yet, Mike?"

Guiltily, still gripping the .22, Michael leapt off the couch as his father stepped into the trailer. Dad stopped, just inside the door, his face going through a complicated series of changes. Michael couldn't have been more flustered, or more guilty, if he had meant to steal the gun, not merely hold it as part of his dream of hunting.

"Just . . . just finished," he stammered. And then, "It's a neat rifle, Dad. Really neat." He turned around and pushed the gun back in the direction of the wall, missing one of the pegs so that it fell off into his hands again, accusing him anew.

His father was at his side in two strides, his face pinched into an angry frown. He took the gun from Michael and replaced it himself, deliberately and emphatically. "Guns aren't to play with, son. I didn't think I'd need to tell you that."

"Oh, I know," Michael answered, trying to sound like someone who would never consider playing, pointing a real gun at wallpaper ducks. "I didn't mean . . . I was just . . ." He stopped, took a deep breath. "I've got my own .22 now. A bolt-action with a scope. Mom and . . . I got it for my birthday last week."

"A gun? Dave Ostrom bought you a gun?" His father looked skeptical, almost as though he suspected Michael of lying. "When I knew him, he was one of the world's great pacifists. Or at least that's the way he acted when he came back from Nam."

"He was. I mean he is," Michael stammered. The last

thing in the world he wanted to do was justify Dave to his father. "He still doesn't like guns, but Mom knew how much I wanted it. How much I wanted to go hunting. Like you and I used to," he concluded, his voice trailing off.

His father continued to stare, his expression dubious, but he said, "So you like to hunt, do you?"

"Well . . ." Michael looked toward the window at the end of the trailer to avoid his father's eyes. Cil was out there turning steaks on a smoking grill. "I haven't had a chance to do any real hunting with my gun yet. Just cleared out some of the pigeons that hang around the machine shed, that's all." He glanced toward his father and away again. "You remember what a nuisance they are."

"Yeah." His dad's voice was grim. "I remember. Only your mother never wanted me to do anything about them. She must have changed."

Not really, Michael thought, but he didn't say that. It didn't seem as though it would help anything.

"Did you bring your .22, then?"

The tone of the question was friendly, but still Michael went cold. He shouldn't have mentioned the gun in the first place. He probably wouldn't have if he hadn't been so flustered. "I couldn't," he tried. "I mean . . . Dave not liking guns and all." He turned up his palms as though the gesture completed his explanation somehow.

His father, however, was clearly waiting for more. For a man who seemed to like to talk, he obviously knew how to keep still when there was something he wanted to hear.

"You see," Michael said finally, feebly, "Dave kind of took it back. The same day he gave it to me, actually."

"Took it back? Your birthday present?"

Michael let indignation push up the volume of his voice. "I hadn't done anything bad with the gun, either. Not one thing!"

"Lord!" Dad turned away, slapping his thigh in disgust. The impact made a sharp crack that filled the small trailer. "What a . . . " He hesitated and then concluded, almost lamely, "jerk!"

Michael was so relieved to see the focus of his father's anger switch from himself to Dave that he felt only vaguely uneasy about the half-truth he had told. He hadn't actually done anything bad *with the gun* , though. Had he?

Shaking his head, his father sat down. He patted the place next to himself on the couch. "Mike," he said when Michael had lowered himself gingerly to the indicated spot, "can you forgive me?"

It was Michael's turn to stare. "Forgive you? For what?"

"For not being there for you all these years. For letting another man take over a job that should have been mine."

Michael's throat went instantly tight. What could he say? *It's all right? I don't mind?* But his father had just named the thing that he minded more than anything else in the whole world.

"It seemed better that way." Dad was fiddling with a raveled thread from the couch upholstery. "Since I couldn't stick the farm, the marriage, it seemed better to let you go. To give somebody else a whack at being your dad. I'm not saying I was right, you understand. But it's the way I was thinking at the time."

Michael nodded, tentatively at first and then with more conviction. He wanted to understand. He truly did. He had always known that his father had agreed to the adoption — he'd had to agree for it to go through — and that was the part that had hurt the most. That his father hadn't cared enough to object.

"But . . . well . . ." Dad lifted his eyes slowly. If Michael hadn't known better, he would have thought his father was pleading. "That doesn't need to keep us from starting over now. Does it, Mike?"

"Of course not!" Michael wanted to laugh and to cry at the same time. He wanted to throw his arms around his father's neck and tell him how long he had been waiting, how often he had dreamed of a moment exactly like this!

But before he could do any of it, his dad sprang up, brushing his hands against one another briskly as if he had just finished handling something old and dusty. "Then that's settled. Good. Now let's have ourselves some dinner." And with a great clatter, he began opening cupboard doors and drawers, taking out plates and glasses and tableware.

Michael got up to help him, his heart brimming with the thousands of questions he needed to ask, the million more things he wanted to tell his father, too. Obviously, though, this wasn't the time.

Cil brought the steak in from outside, along with creamed corn and pork and beans, heated in their open cans on the grill while the steak cooked. At home Michael would have been eating fresh vegetables from his mother's big garden, not canned, and the pork and beans would have been made from scratch, baked all day in the oven. Still, a meal had never looked better.

There was room for only two at the table, so Michael quickly took his plate and went to the couch, leaving the place across from his father to Cil. He didn't want Dad to have to choose, after all.

In all his dreams about being with his father, Michael had never even thought about the possibility of his dad's having a girlfriend, though he undoubtedly should have. After all, his mother had remarried two years after the divorce.

It was all right, though, having Cil here. She was fun, and she and his father joked and teased one another in a way Michael could never remember his parents doing when they were together. In a way his mom and Dave rarely did either, for that matter. Just listening to Cil and his father made Michael feel good. Besides, Cil didn't live here at the trailer. He and his dad would still have plenty of time alone.

But though Michael had talked easily to Cil on the long drive from Denver to Salida, he now found himself unable to locate a single topic of conversation that seemed right for the three of them together. He sat cutting and chewing his steak with infinite care and discarding one opening line after another.

I had a turtle when I was in the third grade. His name was Bo. He hibernated one winter and never woke up.

Apple crisp is my favorite dessert. Hot with cinnamon ice cream melting on it. What's yours?

I made you a set of bookends in shop last year. But then I didn't know where to send them. I still have them, though. At home. I just forgot to bring them.

Do you love me? Did you used to think about me sometimes? Why did it take you so long to call?

"Let me tell you," his father was saying, "about the time I crashed my plane on an ice floe in Bristol Bay." And he spun a long, complicated story that ended with his being snowed in for the winter with an Inuit woman in an igloo.

Michael glanced at Cil, wondering how she felt as his dad told about being with some other woman. But she seemed amused and said only, "You know, Bert, that story gets a bit better every time I hear it." Then she winked at Michael in a way that brought the heat rushing to his face.

Dad tossed back his head and laughed. "That's because a good storyteller knows how to make a few improvements here and there," he said, reaching across the table to lay his hand on top of Cil's. Then he went on to tell about the time he nearly got his throat slit in a poker game in San Antonio.

Michael listened, overwhelmed. What an incredible life his father had lived. What stories could a thirteen-year-old kid ever tell in return that anybody would have the slightest interest in listening to?

"What do you do for fun when you're out with your friends?" Cil asked suddenly, turning to Michael when his dad's tale about the poker game was done.

Michael opened his mouth to respond but found himself without an answer. What did he do for fun? Remembering his friends at home was like trying to recall something from another life.

Before he could manage any kind of reply for Cil, his father posed another question. "I suppose Rob Hansen's kid is one of your pals. What was his name? Neil?"

Michael's heart stopped. Naturally Dad would remember Neil Hansen. He and Neil's dad had been pretty good friends. Michael had almost forgotten that. Still he answered neutrally, "Neil Hansen? Not especially. No."

"Aren't the Hansens still on the next place, just up the highway?"

"Yeah. Sure. But Neil's older than me. He's just finished eighth grade. Besides" — Michael bent over his plate, intent on cutting another piece of steak — "he's a bully."

Michael could feel his father watching him, intently. "Does he bully *you*?" he asked, his voice penetrating but very quiet.

"Not really," Michael answered, though even as he said the words he wondered why he wasn't being honest. Hadn't this been one of the topics he had dreamed of talking to his dad about, how to get guys like Neil Hansen to leave him alone?

"Well," he amended, clearing his throat, "maybe he gets on my case just a little. I'm pretty sure he's the one who stuffed a string of lit firecrackers in my pocket on the last day of school." He reached for a laugh, but when he couldn't find one, he popped the bite of steak into his mouth instead. As he waited for his father to speak he hardly dared to chew.

When his dad's response came, Michael hadn't the slightest idea how to take it. The man gazed at Michael sternly and asked, "Why?"

"Huh?"

"Why?" his father repeated. "Why did you let Neil do such a thing?"

Michael didn't know how to answer a question like that. *A dumb question like that*, he almost found himself thinking. His father's eyes were steady on his face. Michael noticed that they were hazel, like Michael's own.

"I don't let him. He just does! Besides, he's twice as big as me."

His father shrugged. "What difference does that make? Size isn't everything. The bigger they are, the harder they fall."

Michael had heard that one before. Who hadn't? Only what good did it do if you couldn't make them fall? He didn't say that, however.

"Come on now, Bert." Cil's tone was teasing, but her

meaning was perfectly serious. "Don't tell me you didn't get pushed around when you were Mike's age. I spent ten years in junior highs. I know what boys that age are like."

His father flushed, just the slightest touch of red tipping his cheeks and the rims of his ears. "Nobody pushed me around," he answered tersely, glowering at Michael as though he had been the one to suggest such a thing. "Ever!"

Cil looked exasperated, but she said nothing more. She stood and went to the sink to fill a kettle with water from a hand pump.

"I know what it's like," his father continued, more gently, still speaking only to Michael. "I wasn't such a big fellow when I was your age, either. " He let out a single, dry laugh. "I guess in most crowds I'm still not. But I can hold my own. That's what you've got to learn, Mike. To hold your own."

Michael nodded, relief seeping in around the edges. His father was right. Of course. And wasn't that one of the things he had come here to learn, to hold his own? And who better to teach him than his father, who hadn't been "such a big fellow" either?

His dad pushed his plate away, shaking his head. "It's just the way I thought it would be. You need me. That's for sure."

"I do," Michael said softly, but his dad continued without seeming to notice the interruption.

"I've known Dave Ostrom since back when I first

married your mother and moved to Eleva, and I always figured he wouldn't have the slightest idea what to do with a son. Teach you to farm. Sure. But there are more important things a man needs to know than how to pull milk from a cow's teats."

Michael set his plate beside himself on the couch and leaned forward. "What kinds of things?"

Dad made a sweeping gesture with his hands that seemed to take in the whole world, but he said only, "How to face a river like the Arkansas, for one. Running rapids will toughen you up if anything can. You need toughening, Mike. Bullies like Neil Hansen, they can smell fear. They feed on it."

Michael held himself very still. Was that it, the whole thing? Just that he needed to be tough? If he could be *braver* somehow, would the bullies of the world leave him alone? He wasn't sure he believed it.

But his father's face was shining with an almost spiritual light. "Once you've taken on the Royal Gorge," he was saying, "once we've gone through it together, you and me, we'll be father and son again. Just the way it was meant to be. And after that, you'll never be scared of anybody or anything again. I promise."

Vaguely, Michael was aware of Cil. She was standing by the small stove, waiting for the heating kettle. She stood stiffly, her back turned to both of them, studying something off in the distance where the mountains swallowed the last of the evening light. She seemed to be removing herself from the whole conversation, but

Michael didn't care. All he could think about, all he could hear were his father's words. *We'll be father and son again. Just the way it was meant to be.*

And the joy that swam in his eyes blotted out Cil, blotted out everything except the two of them, himself and his father . . . and the promise waiting for them both.

· 9 ·

The first thing Michael noticed when he opened his eyes the next morning was that his father's .22 rifle was gone from the wall. The long, dark shape that had been resting over his bed, glinting dully in the moonlight as he had waited for sleep to come, had vanished.

He sat up, his heart beginning to pound. Had he had the dream again last night? Even here? What had he done with his father's gun?

He leapt out of bed, surveying the trailer wildly. The gun was nowhere to be seen, but the curtain in front of his father's bed was pushed back and the bed neatly made. His father was gone.

Michael sank back to the couch. Then it must have been his dad who had taken the gun. And gone off somewhere.

Without him.

It was then that he saw the note on the table. He picked it up and read it, numbly.

Mike,

You were sleeping so hard, I decided not to wake you. Figured you could probably do with a bit of extra sleep after all your travel. I've gone to work. There's food in the cooler and the cupboard. Have whatever suits you. I've got an all-day trip, so I'll see you about five or five-thirty.

It was signed, *Bert*, then that was crossed through and he had written *Dad* instead.

Five or five-thirty! That was the entire day! Michael stared out the window as though he might find something in that barren landscape to contradict what he had just read.

His father had gone, just left him sleeping! Anger rose in his chest, almost as familiar as breath.

What was Bert Hensley thinking, anyway? That his son had flown all the way to Colorado to spend his days alone in this crummy trailer? Michael kicked the cupboard door in front of him, and the entire trailer reverberated with a hollow metallic sound, like a giant can. He might as well be shut up inside a can for all there was to do around here! There wasn't even electricity to support a television or radio.

And now his father had gone off and left him . . . again!

Not only left him but taken the gun as well! Nobody needed a .22 rifle for whitewater rafting. Obviously his father had figured it wouldn't be safe to leave it behind. Just because he had taken it down last night, just because he had held it, was that reason for his dad not to trust him?

Michael's stomach felt empty and heavy at the same time.

He plodded to the outhouse — another insult, having to use a stinking outhouse — and back again to the trailer. Then, because he couldn't think of anything better to do, he pumped the faucet for water to brush his teeth. Then he pumped a few more times just to watch more water run down the drain. All the water had to be carried to the trailer, and it was a big job. Dad had said so last night. He had warned Michael to be careful about how much he used.

Michael turned away from the sink. It was a stupid thing to do, wasting water. He would probably be the one carrying it next time.

Anyway, he might as well eat breakfast. He took out milk from the cooler and Cheerios from the cupboard. Then he changed his mind. He put those back and selected a bottle of Coors beer, some pepper cheese, and soda crackers instead. He had never drunk beer before, but then his father probably wouldn't care about his trying just one bottle. As usual, he wasn't around to care.

The pepper cheese set Michael's mouth on fire. The Coors put out the fire, but it tasted kind of brown somehow.

Holding the bottle up to the window's light, he decided the stuff looked more like pee. He couldn't figure why some kids at junior high seemed to think beer parties were the ultimate in fun. Not if it meant having to drink the stuff.

Michael took another bite of the hot cheese, followed quickly by a swallow of beer. It was hard to decide which was worse.

He put the cheese back into the cooler, stuffed his mouth with crackers to try to erase the taste, and went outside to pour the rest of the Coors on the ground. Then he looked around for a place to dispose of the bottle. Just in case his dad hadn't quite meant the *whatever* in *whatever suits you.*

He dropped the beer bottle down the hole in the outhouse. It hit bottom with a splushy whump, and Michael hurried back into the sunlight, shuddering.

But then he stopped. What was wrong with him? This was his father he was mad at. The man he'd been longing for, carrying on imaginary conversations with for most of his life. Why, Dad didn't know it, but he had been standing right next to Michael when Rilda had been awarded the blue ribbon at the state fair. Michael hadn't even cared what Dave had said — or not said — afterwards. He hadn't needed to care. In his imagination, his father had said plenty.

Now they were finally together, for real, and he was acting like a spoiled brat.

Despite the blazing sun, he shivered. Sometimes he scared himself with his own rage, as though the dream he'd been having the last few weeks had the power to force itself upon him, even when he was awake.

A large, open-topped Jeep was barreling along the gravel road in front of his dad's place, throwing up a plume of dust, and Michael turned to watch it. As it got closer, he could see that the side of the Jeep said RIVER RAFTERS in large letters, and hope caught suddenly in his throat. His dad had come back for him after all!

The Jeep turned in and bumped toward him, and Michael waited expectantly until the vehicle came to an abrupt halt a few feet from where he was standing. The man at the wheel, however, was definitely not his father.

It doesn't matter, Michael told himself as he walked toward the Jeep, smiling. *Dad sent somebody out here. He was thinking about me, anyway.*

The driver was an old man with wisps of white hair that floated around his head like mist. "You Mike?" he asked. Gummed, rather. He didn't seem to have any teeth.

Michael nodded.

"I'm Sam." It came out *Sham*. "Your daddy asked me to stop by and check on you. See if you was done sleeping."

Was this the best his dad could do? A toothless old man? Still, Michael answered pleasantly enough, "Yeah, I'm done. I must have been really zonked this morning. I didn't even hear my dad leave."

"I was born in this here valley," Sam continued, as though Michael had asked. "Back when the century was new. Lived here all my life." He nodded approvingly at the surrounding ranks of mountains etched against a faultless sky.

Michael wasn't sure what the old man expected him to say. *That's nice?*

But Sam seemed to have his own agenda. He fixed Michael with a penetrating blue stare that made him think, uncomfortably, of Dave and said, "Kind of lonesome, ain't it?"

"Naw," Michael lied. "Besides, I brought some books with me." All he had with him were a couple of old favorites, already read several times. But he didn't want Sam to think — and report back to his father — that he was the kind of kid who would start feeling sorry for himself the moment he was left alone.

Sam shook his head. "Never got into reading much myself. Don't really see the point in it."

Michael let that pass. Actually, he wasn't much interested in Sam's opinion about reading, so he checked out the Jeep instead. He had always wanted Dave to buy one, but Dave wouldn't even consider it. This one was pretty battered, but it was big. It had two roll bars and two rows of seats behind the driver so as to accommodate eight or nine passengers.

"Well?" Sam said, and he sounded impatient, as though he had been waiting all this time for an answer to some question he hadn't even asked. "Do you wanna go?"

"Go? Go where?" Despite his earlier dissatisfaction with being left alone, Michael wasn't sure about going anywhere with this stranger.

"I'm taking a couple loads of tourists into the mountains. We'll visit a ghost town or two. Might even find some gold left behind in one of those abandoned mines!" Sam grinned, and his toothless mouth looked cavernous.

Yeah. Sure we will, Michael thought. Was this what his father wanted, for him to go with Sam? But then he must have, because he was the one who had sent the old man. So Michael shrugged and said, "Okay." He glanced toward the trailer, wondering if there was something he was supposed to lock up, but since he had no key anyway, he climbed into the front seat. The Jeep was moving again before he had gotten properly settled.

"How long you been here?" Sam asked as they jolted back toward the road.

Michael put both hands on the dashboard to keep from flying over (or through) the windshield. "Just since last night."

"How long you stayin'?" Sam asked next. They had lurched back onto the gravel road, and the old man's foot was heavy on the gas.

"Dunno," Michael called over the nearly deafening spray of gravel on the underside of the Jeep. "We haven't decided yet, my dad and me."

Sam grunted, though Michael didn't have the faintest idea what the grunt was supposed to mean.

The old man said nothing further until they had reached an asphalt highway and the worst of the noise had abated. "Didn't know your daddy had a boy," he said then, and Michael jerked back into his seat as if he had been slapped. How could one of his father's friends not know such a thing? "I didn't think he stayed in any one place long enough to see any of his seed come to harvest," Sam added.

Michael stared. Obviously, Sam just didn't know his father very well or else he was getting so old he didn't remember what he'd been told. Michael was sure his dad talked about him, thought about him all the time. "He stayed a whole winter with an Eskimo woman in Alaska," he tossed back. "In an igloo," he added more tentatively because Sam was chuckling.

Michael felt himself blush. He knew his defense was dumb. Besides, his father had lived for a lot longer than that on the farm with his mother and him.

"I've known men like your daddy all my life," Sam said. "He's got an itch. Always running. Always thinking someplace else — or somebody else — is gonna be better." The old man cast a look at Michael. "You like him?"

Michael wasn't sure whether Sam was asking if he *liked* his father or *was like* him, but he answered emphatically, "Of course!" The answer was the same either way.

Sam nodded, apparently satisfied, then added, almost as an afterthought, "He's a good man, your dad."

Michael didn't reply. Why would Sam think he needed to be told? Still, the thing he had said rankled. "Always running." As though his dad was scared. As though a man who could face plane crashes and knife fights over card games and some of the worst rapids in Colorado could possibly be scared.

Sam had lived in this same valley his entire life. He had admitted it right off. Which showed how much he understood about people who were brave enough to go off and start their lives anew the way his dad had done.

The way he, Michael, was doing.

By late afternoon and the end of the second trip, Michael was sure he could have run the excursion himself, except, perhaps, for the driving. And he wasn't so certain he couldn't have done that. Driving a Jeep didn't look that much different from driving a tractor. At least the driver had something solid to hang onto as they bounced crazily up and down these mountains.

To entertain the mers, you started out by saying that you were sorry but you wouldn't be able to talk while the Jeep was moving. You'd forgotten your teeth, so you had no way to strain out the bugs. And then you did things like picking up a pine cone and asking the youngest kid on the tour if she knew what it was. A porcupine egg, you answered yourself. Or you stood next to an abandoned mine shaft with your head cocked and told everyone that if they listened closely enough they were sure to hear somebody down there jabbering in Chinese.

When Sam pulled up at the trailer next to Michael's dad's battered pickup, the old man asked, "Wanna go out again tomorrow?"

Michael's head was pounding and his stomach churning. The lunch of enchiladas Sam had shared with him had been much too hot for his taste, especially after the breakfast he had chosen. It had been preferable, however, to the only alternative offered, an almost black plug of chewing tobacco. And the intense sun and the constant jolting of the Jeep hadn't helped.

"I don't think so," Michael answered politely, climbing out of the Jeep and giving the load of tourists a half wave. "But thanks anyway." A boy about his age, a tourist traveling with his parents, was studying him and the old trailer. The two of them had horsed around a bit during the excursion, and Michael couldn't decide now if the kid was envying him or wondering how anyone could live in such a place.

Sam touched a thumb and forefinger to his forehead, lifting an invisible cap. Then he turned the Jeep abruptly and jolted back toward the gravel road. The tourists clung to one another and to the roll bars as the vehicle careened through a culvert and hit the dusty road, already picking up speed.

Michael struggled with his face as he made his way to the trailer, trying to settle on an expression to hide his feelings about the day. Or to convey them. He wasn't sure which he wanted to do.

His father was rummaging in the food cupboard when Michael stepped through the door. The rifle, he saw immediately, was back in its accustomed place on the wall. Dad spoke without turning to check Michael out. He said, "So you're a beer drinker, are you?"

Michael stopped short, his mouth suddenly bitter again, as though with the long-ago breakfast. He should have known his father would have his bottles of beer counted. Given the way he lived, beer was probably something of a luxury.

"No," Michael answered, his voice flat. "Not really. I just tried one, but I didn't like it very much."

His father turned to face him then. He seemed surprised. Why? Because Michael had told the truth? He said only, "What did you do with the empty?"

"Poured most of it out, and I threw the bottle into the outhouse pit."

His father grimaced. "Marvelous. How'd you like to retrieve it now for the deposit?" But he must have read something in Michael's face, something beyond even his reaction to fishing around in the outhouse pit for a beer bottle, because he went on to say, "Looks like you've had a tough day. Didn't you like riding with Sam?"

"I liked it fine," Michael answered, though he knew his tone belied his words. He might have been talking to Dave, the way he sounded. And then it came out before he had even decided whether he wanted it to or not. "I guess you don't trust me, huh?"

"What do you mean?"

"You took your .22 with you . . . to work. Like you thought I'd shoot somebody or something."

His father didn't reply immediately. "*Should* I trust you?" he asked finally.

Michael faced his father square on, though he

couldn't stop something deep inside from quaking. Did he trust himself? "Yeah," he said, more emphatically than he felt. "You should."

His dad returned his gaze without flinching. Finally he said, "All right, Mike. I apologize. I guess you deserve my trust. But don't let me down. You're not to touch that rifle unless I'm here, unless I say you can. Understand?"

Michael nodded again, still feeling a bit sullen, a bit cheated, though he wasn't sure what it was he had been cheated of. "When am I going to get to go on the river with you, then?" he asked, less because he needed to know than because it was the only thing he could think of to say.

"Will tomorrow do?"

"Tomorrow?" The whole disappointing day dissolved instantly. "Yeah. It'll do fine!"

"Cil and I'll be taking the trainees out for the next two days. They're the ones preparing to be guides. You can go along. We'll do Brown's Canyon and the Royal Gorge." Then his father added, turning back to rummage in the cupboard once more, "And this evening, I thought you and I might try a bit of hunting."

"Hunting!" Michael sank to the couch. It was almost too much.

"If you'd like to, that is."

Michael stood up again, too quickly, so that his head swam. "I'd love it! There's nothing I'd love more!"

Dad had found what he had been searching for in the cupboard. A can of beef stew. "None of the big game is in season right now," he was saying, "but we can always go after jackrabbits."

Jackrabbits! Only that? For an instant Michael was disappointed. He started to sit once more, but then he caught himself. Rabbits would be fine. Really! Toads would have been all right. It was a beginning. And they would be out there together, he and his dad, with a gun.

There would be lots of time later for bigger game, time to prove what Bert Hensley's son was made of.

"If we're hunting rabbit," Michael asked, "why are you getting out the stew?"

His father hesitated, the can still in his hand. He looked thoughtful for a moment, as though the question were giving him some kind of problem. "If you hunt for food," he set the can on the table, "you've got to gut your kill . . . clean it. Cook and eat it, too." He was studying Michael's face. "Think you're up to that?"

For an instant Michael felt again the limp weight of the pigeon in his hand, remembered the blood. Was he? "Sure I am," he said. "I know what hunting's about."

His dad smiled. No, not quite a smile. It was just a muscle that twitched at one corner of his mouth and then went still again. "Jacks move fast. Getting a clean shot at one can be a challenge." He touched the can of stew. "I'll leave this out in case we come home empty-handed."

"I'm a pretty good shot." Michael took a step toward his father. "We won't need that stuff. I'm sure of it!"

His father laughed and moved to meet him, hugging him so hard that Michael could almost feel his ribs pop.

Michael hugged him back with nearly equal strength. He was home . . . at last.

It was almost too good to believe.

· 10 ·

Michael kept by his father's side, matching the man's stride. He carried the gun carefully cradled in his right arm, the safety on, the barrel always pointing to the ground.

Walking through the countryside here was different than it was at home. In the hardwood forests of southeastern Minnesota, the vegetation was so dense that you could barely move through it unless you found a deer path to follow. Here everything was open, the growth spaced out so that the walking would have been easy if it hadn't been for all the cactus and other spiny plants to watch out for.

Though the day had been warm, almost hot, the evening had cooled, and the air was balmy. Michael was acutely aware of his father's presence at his side. He could feel him there without even having to glance in his direction. It was as though he gave out a luminescence or a subtle scent that kept Michael's senses apprised of his nearness.

They had been walking for about ten minutes when the first jackrabbit erupted, almost from beneath Michael's feet, startling him so that he nearly dropped the .22. And then while he was struggling to reestablish his grip, it bounded away on astonishingly long legs. Michael raised the rifle, but much too late to do anything, and lowered it again without having fired.

"That's the way, Mike," his father said. "Hold your fire when you can't get a good shot."

Michael nodded, relieved. His father wasn't going to criticize him, then, either with words or silently. Not like Dave. And not like Michael's mother, either, who would have made a big deal out of it, asking him how he was feeling, whether he was disappointed about missing his first chance. With his father it was all very matter-of-fact. Just two men talking.

Michael snapped the safety back on and handed the gun over. That was what they had agreed before they started. They would take turns, and your turn meant you sighted a rabbit, whether you got off a shot or not.

He and his father resumed walking, Michael swiveling his head slowly and constantly to scan everything within range. He wanted to be ready, even when he wasn't carrying the gun. That first one had disappeared so quickly! Jackrabbits were clearly faster than the cottontails at home.

There was another flurry of activity, the flash of a black tail, and a brown-gray form appeared for just an instant before it blended into the surrounding vegetation. His father fired, missed, and handed the gun back to Michael without comment.

Michael tried to think of something to say, something companionable like what his dad had said to him.

"Good try," he offered, but the hesitation before he spoke made the words come out seeming limp and out of place.

Still Dad said, "Thanks." He never seemed to be bothered by, or apparently even to notice, Michael's awkwardness.

They walked on, and Michael held the gun firmly, carefully. A light breeze had sprung up, playing against his skin. He felt as though he were walking in a trance. All those years of dreaming about hunting with his father again. And here they were at last, a gun between them and the long summer's evening stretching before them.

A ground squirrel scurried past, and Michael smiled after it. How perfect this moment was! The entire day hadn't been so bad, really. Even toothless Sam had been kind of interesting. And tomorrow Michael and his dad would be out on the river together. Brown's Canyon and the Royal Gorge!

The next jackrabbit emerged from behind a spiny yucca plant. It hopped a few feet, and then as though it had come for this purpose, like the buck so many years before, it froze. Michael had time to click off the safety, to sight, to fire, and to fire again just as the jack took off, untouched and startled by the first sharp report of the gun.

Michael watched in amazement as the animal, practically in flight an instant before, turned a spinning somersault in the air and landed in a sprawled heap. Only after it landed, it didn't go still as a person had a right to expect. It didn't even seem to know it had been hit. Or somehow knew and refused to believe. Crazily, the rabbit continued to try to run, its strong hind legs jerking, its front paws scrabbling at the ground.

Michael pointed the gun and fired again. And again. And again.

"Whoa, Mike."

It was only when his father put a hand on his arm to stop him that Michael realized he had been shooting with his eyes closed. Guiltily, he lowered the rifle.

His father kept his hold on his arm. "Sometimes there are nerves that go on responding after you've made your kill."

"Oh." Michael felt foolish.

Dad walked over to the limp jackrabbit, and Michael followed. However, he didn't bend down to examine it when his father did. He found himself remaining stiffly upright, studying the mountains in the distance. In the crevice formed by two peaks the last of an elongated figure of snow was left.

On the ride from the airport, Cil had told him the melting shape was called the angel of Shavano and that this summer it was taking longer to disappear than usual. Shavano had been a medicine man and war chief, and the angel named after him was supposed to watch over the residents of Salida. Apparently, though, angels didn't do such a good job with rabbits.

"Good shooting." His father lifted the limp carcass to demonstrate a dark hole at the top of the shoulder.

"Looks like you must have shattered the spine with that second shot."

Michael looked, then turned his head away quickly. He had to get hold of himself. He was going to spoil everything.

Dad laid the rabbit on the ground again and straightened up, the beginnings of a smile crinkling the corners of his eyes. "It's just as well the rest of your shots missed. There wouldn't have been much left for eating if you'd connected every time."

Michael could feel the familiar heat flooding his face. He wondered if he would ever grow past blushing, if he would ever be able to take teasing without turning on like a stoplight. Like some silly girl. At least his father didn't know — couldn't possibly know — how wildly he had been shooting.

"I just have one suggestion, Mike."

Michael forced himself to look directly into his father's widening grin.

"Next time you might want to try it with your eyes open." And he began to laugh.

Michael forced himself to join in the laughter, but the sound of his own voice was rusty and strained. To cover it, he bent down and examined his kill.

The jack was larger than Michael had expected, much bigger and more lean than the rabbits they had at home, and the ears were enormous. There was nearly as much length in the long, delicate ears as there was in the rabbit itself.

"Jackrabbits are really hares," his father was explaining, squatting next to him now, "not rabbits. See that split in the lip?"

Michael saw.

"That's where we get the term 'harelip.' All hares have that opening. And they don't live in burrows like rabbits do, either."

Michael reached out with a tentative finger and touched the rabbit . . . the hare. It was warm, as he had expected, but something about the soft fur and the still-pliable flesh startled him. He jerked his finger back as if he had been burned.

And yet there was another kind of reaction gathering in his chest. Something entirely different from the guilty caution of his first approach. It was a sense of power. *He* was the one who had killed this creature. It was lying here dead because of *him*. A minute ago it had been alive, running, in charge of itself, and now it was . . . his. His prey. His supper.

And his father's, too, of course.

"Do you have a knife?" he asked.

His father drew a slender knife from a sheath at his belt and handed it to Michael. There was the same studying look in his eyes that Michael had so often seen there in the last twenty-four hours. Was he thinking his son was going to back out? Well, he had another think coming.

Michael lifted the dead rabbit by its long, supple ears and stretched it out on the ground in front of himself. He gripped the knife.

He had lived all his life with death, with knowing that the steaks and hamburgers on his plate had once been cattle, probably ones he had cared for and fed . . . and sometimes even loved. If you ate meat, animals had to die. It was that simple. Only on a farm today, somebody else did the killing, the cutting. The animals went away in a truck, and they came back wrapped in small white packages, just the right size to tuck into the freezer, to fit into the roaster or the frying pan.

His father was waiting, saying nothing.

Michael swallowed. He had never done such a thing before, but that didn't mean he couldn't. "Where do I start?" he asked.

Dad told him, and he plunged the sharp blade through the thick, soft fur.

· 11 ·

Michael sat examining his fork. The piece of jack-rabbit on it looked like meat, any ordinary meat.

His dad was still watching him, as he had watched through the entire process of skinning and gutting the rabbit. (Michael didn't know where the phrase *as easy as skinning a rabbit* had come from. It hadn't seemed so easy to him.) His father had taken over only to show him where the glands were that had to be removed to keep the meat from taking on a strong taste.

And Michael had done it all. Except he had declined to be shown how to cure the skin so he would be able to keep the fur as a souvenir. He had thrown the bloody skin aside, but he had managed everything else. Even had supervised the meat as it browned on the grill.

Now he sawed at the leg on his plate. It looked much like a chicken leg, cooked without skin, but there was a resistance to it that didn't bode well for the eating. He might have been trying to cut through a mass of rubber bands.

He got a small piece separated finally, but left it on his plate and took a bite of his bread instead. That was all they were having for supper, the grilled jackrabbit and white, grocery-store bread. Mom would have had a fit about its not being a balanced meal, but he didn't care.

His father was drinking a beer, sitting back from the table as though still waiting for supper to be delivered. He had buttered his slice of bread, but he hadn't yet touched the meat on his plate. "You've done some growing up since the last time you and I went hunting," he said in an approving voice.

His head bent over his plate, Michael concentrated on cutting another bite, though he hadn't eaten the first one yet. Who didn't do a lot of growing up between five and thirteen? Still, he waited hopefully for his father to enumerate the ways he had changed.

Dad blew into the half-empty beer bottle, making a soft, hooting note. When he finally spoke again, it was only to say, "I guess I should have realized back then."

"Realized what?" Michael prompted.

"That you were too young. Your mother tried to tell me, but I wouldn't listen." He shook his head, chuckling in a way that didn't sound particularly amused. "It never occurred to me, though, that you'd take it the way you did!"

A cold hand was gripping Michael's heart, but the question had to be asked. He had to know what his father was talking about. He formed the words carefully. "Are you talking about the day we went hunting?"

His father nodded slightly.

"What did I do?"

Dad put the beer bottle down and leaned toward him. "You don't remember?"

"I remember sitting with you in the stand. I remember shooting the deer. My finger was on top of yours on the trigger. But . . ." He shrugged. "That's all." *You laughed*, he almost added, but then he didn't. Maybe he was wrong about that.

His father was watching him so intently that Michael had to hold himself rigid to keep from squirming in his seat. Finally Dad spoke, in a teasing voice. "So you don't remember trying to kill your old man, huh?"

"I did what?" A wave of nausea made Michael release his fork. It clattered to his plate.

"Then you *have* forgotten. Curious you'd forget that when you remember the rest."

Michael could only sit there, helpless, waiting to hear. It was worse, even, than he had thought!

"When I was gutting the buck, you started to bawl. It's a bloody job, you know, but it didn't seem to be just that." His father smiled, shook his head. "You decided we'd shot one of Santa's reindeer, and you wanted him put back. Made alive again, you know? When I told you it couldn't be done, you went crazy. Why, you went after me with a dead branch."

He brushed one hand over the back of his head as though he could still feel the effects of the attack. "If you'd been any bigger, I believe you'd have knocked my head off."

Michael gripped the edge of the table, trying to slow the spinning in his brain. He had hit his father with a dead branch? No wonder the man had gone away!

Dad didn't seem to notice his reaction. He continued to explain, his tone caught somewhere between accusation and admiration. "You came up behind me with this . . . well, it was practically a log. It was almost as big as you were! And you whacked me good. 'Leave Santa's reindeer alone!' you were yelling. 'Leave him alone!' I was plenty surprised, I can tell you!"

Michael didn't know what to say, how to defend himself, where to begin to apologize for so terrible a thing. So he said, totally inconsequentially, "I was five years old and I still believed in Santa Claus? I must have been a pretty stupid little kid." After all, Kari had figured out the Santa bit a year or more ago . . . with just a little help from him.

"Not stupid. Just sensitive, I guess. And young. At least that's what your mother said."

Strangely, Michael still couldn't remember. Nothing about Santa's reindeer, about trying to attack his father. And if that was what had happened, why had his father laughed? Had it been so funny, seeing a little kid trying to protect something he believed in?

"That was why you left, wasn't it? Because I hit you." Michael said it quietly, but with dead certainty. It was what he had always known, after all.

"No! Of course not!" Dad pulled himself upright, glaring as though he had been the one accused. "It wasn't because of that. It wasn't even because of the fight your mom and I had when you and I got back home. She thought it was my fault that you were so upset. She said I never should have taken you hunting in the first place, and she was probably right. But it was just . . . the last straw. You know?"

Michael didn't know.

His dad reached across the table and took hold of his wrist. "It was only a very small piece of everything she and I had been fighting about for years, of everything that didn't work between us."

When Michael still didn't respond, he shook his arm, almost roughly. "If that's what you've been thinking, that my going away had anything to do with you, you can stop. Now. It was us. Your mom and me. Both of us."

Michael's wrist was beginning to ache from the pressure of the grip, but he didn't try to pull away.

"And the farm," his father added. "Me not liking to be stuck there with all those damn cows. It was lots of stuff really. In fact, I'd say you were about the only wholly good thing your mother and I had going for us."

He released his hold then, and Michael exhaled, a long, slow expulsion of air. The relief that came with the release of that breath was so enormous that he picked up his fork and took the bite of meat waiting there on his plate.

He was still chewing, several minutes later, when his father exploded into laughter. He thumped his beer bottle down on the table and threw back his head and roared.

Michael sat up straight, his jaws still working, the sound of his father's mirth an electric current applied to an old wound.

Dad pushed his plate aside as though he needed space for the words that were about to come. When he finally could say something Michael could understand, however, it was only, "Tough, isn't it?"

By this time Michael had swallowed the meat in a tasteless, fairly whole lump. "Yeah," he said, confusion filling him. "Kind of. Maybe I didn't cook it right. Or I did something wrong when I was cleaning — "

"Nope." His father shook his head, still laughing, wiping his eyes. "You cleaned it just fine. You're not a bad cook, either. But jackrabbit's hardly fit to feed a dog. The cowboys used to be ashamed if someone came across one of them eating a jack. It proved what poor hunters and trappers they were that they couldn't get anything better."

Michael held himself perfectly still, waiting to understand. Why had his father let him skin the jackrabbit, gut it, cook it, then?

"They're varmints, really. They're taking over. I go out and shoot them just for practice, to rid the country of them."

"But . . . but you told me to . . ." He couldn't finish.

"You were the one who assumed we were going to eat what we killed. I just went along with it." His father stood up. He took his plate and Michael's and dropped the carcass — somehow it no longer looked like meat — into a garbage sack.

Michael was awash with confusion. He couldn't think of anything to say except simply, "Why?"

Dad had taken out a can opener and was opening the

can of stew instead, the one he had laid out earlier in case they came home without game. "I hadn't planned it, but when you said what you did about eating the jacks, I needed to see if you would, if you could. If you're going to hunt, you've got to be able to take it the whole way. I don't like to see people who want someone else to do the dirty work for them after they're through killing."

Michael stared at his father. So he had been testing him. To see if he was still the kid he'd taken hunting before. The kid who helped to pull the trigger and then bawled, blamed his father for the death.

"Did I do okay?" he asked, his voice pinched and raw.

"Okay?" Dad dumped the stew into a saucepan and lit one of the gas burners on the stove. He turned back to Michael, his eyes still filled with laughter . . . and something more than laughter. "You did better than okay, Mike. I'm real proud of you, son."

Michael could find no words to reply. What was wrong with a test when you came out of it so well? His dad was proud of him.

The happiness made a great lump in his throat, and he could only nod and smile . . . and smile and nod some more. He had done the right thing, the thing that would please his father.

At last.

"Thanks," he said quietly, and, glowing with pleasure, he sat back to wait for the stew.

·12·

Michael stood on the bank of the Arkansas River in the circle of trainees, listening to the safety talk his father was delivering. "I know you've all heard this before, but listen up again," his father had commanded at the beginning. And the trainees were listening.

But Michael hadn't heard any of it before, and he attended the most intently of anyone, repeating parts to himself silently.

High side. If the boatman called *high side* it meant the inflatable raft was caught on a rock and about to capsize. Everyone was to go to the high side of the raft immediately. The intention was to shift the raft so it would come off the rock . . . right side up.

Michael kept glancing over at the river. It was hard to see what all the commotion was about. The Arkansas River was shallow and narrow. Hardly a *river*, really. At least not to someone who had grown up near the Mississippi. Actually, it didn't look any bigger or more fierce than the Root River that passed along the edge of their farm. And the only time the Root River was more than a wide, meandering creek was when it flooded occasionally in the spring.

"Remember," his father was saying, "the boat is number one. As long as you're in the boat, you're number one as well. If you fall out, we'll try to get you, but the welfare of the boat always comes first. If you're in the water, you're number two." Was he looking in Michael's direction as he spoke? Michael tightened the buckles on his life vest.

His father began sorting the dozen young men and women who were in training to be guides into two different rafts. Michael stood on one foot, then on the other, waiting for his assignment. There were so many instructions, so many warnings. Despite his assessment of the river, he was beginning to grow uneasy.

"Just my son and Cil in my raft," Dad announced. "We'll be taking the lead."

How Michael loved that . . . *my son!* He was certain some of the young people looked at him with envy, thinking him lucky to be the son of such a man. Bert Hensley was clearly liked and admired here.

Whatever happened, he was going to make his father proud. Yesterday was only the beginning of proving how different he was from the crybaby five-year-old kid his dad had left behind.

"Do you think Mike is dressed warmly enough?" Cil asked, checking out his cutoffs and T-shirt as she climbed into the bow of the boat. "Maybe he should have a wet suit . . . or at least a wool sweater." She was wearing something that looked like tights with what appeared to be boxer shorts over them.

His dad barely glanced at him. "He'll be fine," he replied, to Michael's relief. After all, he was wearing shorts and a T-shirt, too. And then he added, stepping into the raft himself and settling into the rowing position, "Will you push us off, Mike?"

Michael pushed off and clambered into the boat, wet to the knees. The water was cold, a breath-stealing, bone-penetrating cold that he hadn't expected, but the sun was as bright as it had been the day before. He would warm up quickly enough. What was it about women that they were always worrying about what other people were wearing, eating, doing?

Michael settled into the bow just across from Cil and tossed her a smile. He felt victorious over escaping her mothering but pleased to have her there, nonetheless.

She smiled back. Her hair was caught into a long tail this morning, but the coppery curls were already pulling loose and springing around her face in a way that made Michael catch his breath and look off in the other direction.

The current seized the raft immediately, though his father directed their movement with firm, seemingly casual strokes. Facing forward, he guided them toward the middle of the river, and the other two rafts followed. Michael hadn't realized when he had been standing on the shore how swift the current was. This water tumbling down from the mountains moved much faster than the Root River. Faster than the Mississippi, too, for that matter.

Cil and Michael, sitting in the bow, would be doing "paddle assist through the tight spots," Dad had explained. Michael wasn't sure what "a tight spot" looked like, but he planned to be ready when they encountered one.

Cil would take her turn at rowing, too, especially on the second day, when Dad would be checking her out in the Royal Gorge. His father hadn't said anything about Michael's getting a chance to row, and now that he could see how swift the river was, he was just as glad. There would be plenty of time for that later in the month . . . or even later in the summer. His father hadn't said anything about his staying longer, but Michael was sure he would agree.

As they moved into the middle of the river, Michael grasped the T-grip of his paddle and gazed, first at the blue sky — bluer than any Minnesota sky, surely — and then at the swift, brown water itself. This was going to be great. Absolutely great! His feet were cold, but that didn't matter. He and his dad didn't have to be *comfortable* every moment of their lives.

"You'll remember this first time for the rest of your life, Mike," Cil said to him. Michael nodded to her happily.

He was sure she was right. And his father would remember it, too, because Michael was going to make him so proud that he would never want to be separated from his son again. He, Michael, would do everything, absolutely *everything* right.

They hit a series of ripples in the water, and the inflated raft undulated with the changing surface, causing Michael to reach for the safety line that ran across the bow.

"No hanging on," his father barked. "You can't be ready to paddle when I need you if you're holding onto the rope."

Michael dropped the line, flushing. Still, he told himself, he was bound to make a few mistakes. It would be the way the total day came out that really mattered.

"The paddling will hold you in when the water gets rough," Cil told him in a voice meant just for him. Michael nodded a silent thanks, grateful for her ability to know exactly what it was he needed to hear.

"And when I tell you to do something," Dad continued, "do it in time with Cil and only as much as I say. Exactly. If I say two strokes forward, don't decide to do three. An extra stroke could throw us into a rock or a wall."

Michael nodded again and held the T-grip of his paddle more tightly. This was beginning to sound more complicated than he had expected. More dangerous, too. He checked out the rafts following them. The trainees seemed to be having a good time. Except for the ones rowing, they were sprawled casually around their rafts, laughing and calling to one another. And Cil, just across from him, was clearly relaxed and enjoying the river and the balmy, sunshiny day. She held her paddle lightly across her lap. Michael made himself loosen his own grip.

His father and Cil tossed comments back and forth, teasing one another the way they had at supper the first evening. Cil called Michael's dad "T.L.," which was, it turned out, simply short for trip leader. She said it, however, in a slightly mocking tone which made it clear that, while she respected his skill, she wasn't one to bow to authority . . . even his. Dad, in turn, called Cil a "lily dipper." And she explained to Michael, when he asked, that a lily dipper was "someone who doesn't bury the blade of the paddle. They're along for a free ride."

Michael nodded, but he knew full well that whatever Cil might be, she was certainly no "lily dipper."

It was all in good fun, though, and he began to wish his dad would come up with a name for him. Even a derogatory name would please him. Or at least he thought it would.

"This is the Upper Canyon Doors," Dad announced as they came into their first patch of rough water. "We're entering Brown's Canyon."

Despite the sudden turbulence, Michael was surprised to discover how smooth the ride was. Instead of cutting through the river or banging off the top of it the way other kinds of boats would have, the buoyant raft conformed to the water's shape and flow.

"Go loose," Cil told him, just as they entered the rapids. "Ride with it."

And Michael did, allowing his body to shape itself to the raft's movement. As they slid through the froth, though, he couldn't help remembering his father's words: *The boat is number one. If you're in the water, you're number two.*

"Lower Canyon Doors," Cil called as they surfed a wave and ran along close to a rocky wall. Michael tried to lean away from the wall without appearing to do so. If hanging on wasn't allowed, perhaps shifting away from obstacles wasn't either.

And then Cil called again over the increasing din of the water, "And this is Pinball Rapid."

The river seemed to bend, narrow, and divide over a huge rock, all in the same spot. The water roared and splashed into the boat, stinging cold.

"Paddle forward, two strokes," Dad ordered. "Now again . . . two more," and Michael was intrigued to discover that Cil had been right. Pulling against the water with his paddle did hold him firmly into the raft. Or at least it did until they came up against a rock, hard, and Michael toppled over sideways into the soft bottom of the boat. Even as he went down, he could hear his father laughing.

"A carp!" his father shouted, loudly enough that Michael wondered if the boats following could hear, even over the booming water. "Mike's a carp, flopping around in the bottom of the boat!"

Cil reached over to help him up, but Michael pretended not to see her hand. He repositioned himself as quickly as possible and avoided looking back at his father. At least he had a name. He tried to feel grateful for that.

The river was quieter now, and they floated on silently except for the sound of oars dipping into the water and emerging again, then slipping into the water once more. Michael kept watch for more rapids. By the end of the day he intended to have earned an entirely different name — that was for sure!

He could hear the next set of rapids they approached long before he could see them. The water tumbling over the rocks sounded like a freight train.

"This is Zoom Flume," his father announced, and he began to give instructions for negotiating it. Michael wedged himself tighter into the crevice between the tube he was sitting on and the outer tube, licked his dry lips, and held his paddle at the ready.

"Paddle forward," Dad commanded. "Three times. Now one more. Back! Back! Two times back! Now forward again. Two."

Michael was paddling, his head down, watching the movement of Cil's arms out of the corner of his eye to keep pace with her. They slipped through the roaring, foaming water, past enormous boulders waiting to catch and upend their boat. And they came out on the other side as smoothly and easily as if they had just gone down a children's sliding board.

"A great run!" Cil raised her dripping paddle above her head.

"Perfect!" Dad yelled at the same time. He was still rowing, still maneuvering the raft through water that, while quieter now, was never totally calm, seldom entirely unobstructed.

"That's because we've got a super boatman," Cil announced, turning a luminous smile on his father.

"That's because I've got a super crew," he replied, and the smile he flashed back included Michael.

Michael's knees were weak. Whitewater rafting was more exciting, even, than hunting. More scary, too.

But he knew in that moment, beyond any doubt, that there was nothing on earth he wanted more than to stay on with his father and learn to be as super a boatman as he was.

·13·

hey went through Big Drop Rapid and the Widow
Maker, Raft Ripper and Slydell's Suckhole. Each
rapid was different, unique, demanding alertness and
expertise from the boatman. The rush of chilling
water, jagged rocks, sudden drops — none of it became
routine, or felt as if it could ever become routine. After
the first hour, however, the excitement began to lose
some of its dimension of terror. In the quiet spots
between the rapids, Michael found himself looking forward, eagerly, to the next bit of action.

They stopped for lunch along the bank — sandwiches and potato chips and a flavorless red drink the
trainees called "red death." Michael was chilled
through from the repeated wetting and stretched out
gratefully in the sun on a warm boulder. He wouldn't
have dreamed of admitting his discomfort, though.

His dad and Cil sat side by side, and Michael couldn't
help studying them. They made an odd-looking couple. Next to Cil's height and her large frame, his father
seemed even smaller than he was.

Maybe Cil and his dad would marry one day. Michael

could think of worse things than having Cil for a step-mother. But then maybe she wouldn't qualify as a step-mother since his father had given up his parental rights. Was it possible for someone to be de-adopted?

"What was the worst time you ever had on the river?" one of the trainees asked, and that started a whole series of stories. His dad and Cil talked about having entire loads "dump trucked" (the passengers all going out while the raft remained upright), about being flipped, caught on rocks, pulled into whirlpools, and on and on. Listening, Michael felt his arms prickle into gooseflesh despite the penetrating warmth of the sun.

"And then there was the time that I saved your life," Cil reminded his dad, tossing her head back and laughing. A deep hollow at the base of her throat pulsed with the laughter, and Michael found himself unable to take his eyes from the smoothness of that small, concave place.

His dad shot her a look Michael couldn't quite interpret. Annoyed, maybe. Mildly embarrassed, at least. "It wasn't exactly my *life* at stake," he told her.

But Cil didn't seem to be concerned with his reaction. "Oh, I see! Then you actually prefer doing The Numbers out in front of the raft?" She smiled at Michael, inviting him to join in her amusement, but he looked off in the other direction, unwilling to be included in this game. Sometimes he sensed a tension between Cil and his dad that made him itch.

He knew what "The Numbers" were. He had heard

some of the trainees talking about them earlier. They were a series of really tough rapids, too erratic to be used for commercial passengers.

"What happened?" one of the trainees asked, and they all leaned forward to listen to the answer. Michael found himself leaning forward, too.

His father shrugged. *It was no big deal!* the shrug said, but then he went on to answer anyway. "Cil and I and some others from the staff were running The Numbers last summer, and I got dumped from the stern." He leaned forward, his face growing more intense as he got into his own story. "The water was high and the current really boiling. The first thing I know, I'm under the raft instead of following after it like you'd expect. It's real quiet under there, real . . ."

"Dangerous," someone supplied in a low voice, and everyone looked solemn, intent.

"When I finally came up again, I popped out in front of the raft instead of behind. So I looked up, and there's this woman, this quick-thinking guide" — he gave Cil a playful shove — "staring down at me like she's never seen a man in the water before."

Cil took up the story. "I didn't even know he'd gone for a swim! Here I am, paddling along, and suddenly, right under my nose, there's this fellow I'd last seen in the back of the raft!"

"Some guys'll do anything to get you to notice them," commented a small, pert girl with dark eyes and a trilling laugh.

Cil nodded her agreement to the girl and continued.

"So I looked back. I thought maybe it was his twin I was seeing, and I figured one of Bert Hensley was all anybody needed at a time. But his place was empty."

"And having decided it was really me," Michael's dad concluded, "she reached down and plucked me out of the water, like a mother picking up a baby out of a bath." He said it triumphantly, as though the victory of the moment were his, grinning at Cil. "That's when I fell in love," he concluded, and he reached for Cil's hand.

Everyone applauded, including Michael, and Cil gave his dad a big kiss. They applauded the kiss, too.

"You'd better watch out, Mike," one of the boys said. "Dangerous things can happen to you on the river!"

"Yeah," his father added. "I've been stuck with this woman ever since!"

Cil cuffed him playfully.

"Mike Hensley," a girl called from the other side of the large circle, and it took Michael a couple of beats to realize she was speaking to him. He had been Michael Ostrom for so long that the old name hardly seemed his any longer.

"Yeah?" he said.

"Where do you live? When you're not here with your dad, I mean."

"A dairy farm in southeastern Minnesota," he replied, hoping they would ask him more. He could tell them about Rilda, about winning a blue ribbon at the state fair. And then his dad would have a chance to hear, too. He hadn't yet asked anything about the farm.

"I grew up on a farm," a freckled boy announced, and Michael smiled in his direction. Here was someone who would be interested. But then the boy added, "Was I ever glad to get out of there!"

"Tell them the name of the town nearest you," his father prompted, and though Michael was puzzled as to why he wanted him to do that, he complied.

"Eleva."

Everyone seemed to be waiting for something more, and Dad supplied it. "You want to hear how Eleva got its name?"

They all waited . . . except Michael. He knew the story, though he had never known if it was really true or if it was just one of those things somebody made up after the fact. Why had his father brought up that old business, anyway?

"A fellow was painting the grain elevator," his dad continued, "back when a grain elevator was just about all there was to the place. He got as far as E-L-E-V-A when a storm came up, so he climbed down and never returned to finish the job. The name stuck."

Everyone laughed. Even Michael joined in . . . a little, though he wasn't really amused.

How could he have forgotten? His dad had grown up in Minneapolis, and he had always hated the farm, hated Eleva. Now that he thought about it, he could remember Dad saying, more than once, *I'm not going to spend the rest of my life tied to a cow's teats!* The words had always given him such a curious picture of his father, attached to a cow's underside. Michael sifted through his mind for some kind of sharp response to the Eleva story, but he found none.

He was glad a few moments later when his dad announced it was time to get back on the river. The last turn of the conversation had left him feeling curiously disloyal, as though he, too, hated cows. It wasn't hard, though, to see why someone would prefer guiding river rafts to farming. Anyone except Dave, maybe . . . and his mother.

The afternoon's run was as exciting — and as smoothly executed — as the morning's. Cil and his dad took turns rowing, and it was great to have his dad in the bow next to him when Cil was the boatman.

Michael hated to see the end of the day come. They had another full day of rafting ahead of them, though. He reminded himself of that. They would be camping beside the river that night, not even going back to the trailer.

Michael sat loosely in the bow of the raft, his paddle across his lap. He was relaxed, satiated with sun and water. His father was rowing again, the last of the big action behind them for the day. In fact, the river at this point was nearly smooth. There was a large rock to be avoided, but plenty of room. Dad didn't even call for paddle assist.

"What do you think, Cil? Shall we catch that eddy?" his father asked, and Michael looked to see what he might be speaking of. There was nothing on the surface of the river except for what appeared to be a lazy swirl on the downriver side of the rock.

Cil turned in place, frowning, but his father was already pulling toward the rock. Michael leaned out slightly to see what it was he was supposed to catch.

"Bert, I don't think — " Cil began, but she didn't have a chance to finish. They had slipped behind the rock, and the boat seemed to pause, almost to shudder . . . just before it began to spin. As it spun, it pulled downward, filling with water, the river sucking at it, closing in. The water rushed over the sides as though there were no sides there.

It all happened so fast, and yet Michael watched, immobilized, like someone observing the action in a slow-motion film. He might already have been separate from the moment, looking back on it, studying it.

He started to drop his paddle in order to grab for the rope on the submerging bow, but then he remembered. *Never hold the rope!* That's what his father had told him. And so he grasped the paddle more firmly instead, waiting for instructions.

And that was when the raft disappeared from beneath him. It was simply gone, and he found himself afloat. And then no longer afloat but, despite his life jacket, being sucked under sharply. The water closed over his head, and his ears were singing the way they would if he had jumped off a high diving board into a very deep, very cold pool.

Only he hadn't jumped. He hadn't done anything. Just been sitting there, and it was as though the river had reached up and grabbed him. And pulled him down. And imprisoned him there, a giant hand grinding him into the rocky riverbed.

Michael held his breath, though he knew it was no use. He would have to breathe sometime, and the river was never going to let him go. When he had to breathe, finally, there would be only water. When he opened his eyes, there would be nothing but water to see. When his father found him, he would be dead.

He thought of his mother, his gentle mother. He thought of Kari in her flower-sprigged nightgown. He thought of Nipper, the grizzled mongrel who was as old as he, and of Rilda, his red Guernsey cow. Strangely, he thought even of Dave, though he didn't know what it was he thought of Dave. Dave taking possession of his .22? Dave standing watch while Neil Hansen beat him up?

The river was everywhere, pounding at him, pulling on him, and he was struggling, though it was perfectly clear that the struggle wasn't going to help. It was like going up against ten bullies, a hundred. He clamped his mouth shut, still holding his breath . . . uselessly. He wanted to scream for his father, for air.

This can't be happening, he thought. *I'm just a kid. I've barely had a chance to begin.*

And then, as swiftly and emphatically as it had pulled him down, the river spat him out again. He bobbed to the surface like an inflatable toy and found himself, still gripping the paddle, being propelled downstream in the wake of the foundering raft.

His father and Cil were still in the boat. The river hadn't gotten them. And they were watching . . . cheering. Watching and cheering him. So were the trainees, off to one side, far away from the rock and its treacherous water. Paddles were raised, people were yelling.

"Look at that!" his father shouted. "He didn't even lose his paddle!" Michael kicked with all his remaining strength until he got near the raft, and then his dad reached out, grabbed his life vest, and pulled him in.

Lying on his back in the swamped boat, the paddle still clenched in his grip, Michael gazed into the face of the man who had saved his life.

Then he turned on his side and wept.

· 14 ·

The campfire crackled and blazed, but no matter how close he sat, Michael couldn't seem to stop shivering. Even the sweater Cil had loaned him, a wool pullover that hung down almost as long as a dress, didn't help . . . at least not enough.

The hot meal — canned stew again — had warmed him for a little while. Maybe it would have made a bigger difference if he had been able to eat more, but he had managed only half a bowl. At home they referred to any kind of canned meat as "dog food," and enthusiasm for canned stew two evenings in a row was more than he could muster, even when there was no other choice.

Michael had spent the evening feeling equally foolish and brave, a flawed hero. He might have found it easier to accept the good-natured teasing about his "swim" if it hadn't scared him as thoroughly as it had, if he hadn't cried. As it was, he felt too astonishingly alive, too grateful for breath and for his father's gallant rescue to be able to join in the friendly laughter.

He was doubly grateful that no one, especially his father, had mentioned his tears.

People were beginning to lay out their sleeping bags for the night. Michael stood up, stiffly. He had to locate his dad or Cil, find out where his own sleeping bag was. They had "gone for a walk" shortly after supper. At least that's what they had said. He shouldn't think of it that way, though. They probably *were* walking.

And what difference did it make if they were doing something else?

Except that the possibility made a knot clench inside his gut. He didn't know what it was or why, really. He wasn't a little kid to be jealous or anything like that. Besides, he didn't even know whom he would be jealous of. His dad for having Cil or Cil for having his dad?

It was just that this evening there was something he hadn't noticed before between his father and Cil, something from which he felt entirely excluded. No matter how nice they were — and they had both paid extra attention to him all evening — he had felt it the whole time. Something unsaid. Something that was waiting for time alone before it could happen.

He wrapped his arms around himself and began walking. The air was dry and cold. Like fall, not early summer. A pale, egg-shaped moon blotted out most of the stars and flooded the countryside with its thin, white light.

Michael had gone only a short distance down the river from the campsite before he found them. His dad and Cil were indistinct gray silhouettes sitting on a rock along the bank. Talking. Just that. Their backs to him.

Michael sighed with a relief he hadn't known he was feeling.

He was approaching from behind, and though he wasn't trying to be quiet, it was clear they hadn't heard him yet. As he drew closer, he could hear Cil speaking, a sharp edge in her voice. "I still think it was a dirty trick," she was saying.

Michael started to clear his throat, to warn them of his presence, but his father's answer made him stop before the sound had escaped.

"Aw, come on, Cil. The kid's gotta learn."

"Learn what? Not to trust his own father?"

Michael's joints went soft. What did she mean? And who were they talking about? Not him. It couldn't be him. Of course he trusted his father! If he couldn't trust his own father, who else was there?

"I don't know why you're making such a big deal out of the whole thing." Dad was sounding irritated again, the way he had at lunch, only more so. "He wasn't hurt. I knew he wouldn't be. The river was open below there. No rocks. That kind of thing feels a lot worse than it really is. You know that perfectly well."

"I also know you scared him half to death! And for no good reason!"

His father put an arm around Cil's waist. Even in the vague light, his arm looked puny there. "Come on, Cil," he said. "I had my reasons. You've gotta see that. Mike needs toughening up. He's a wimp, for God's sake. The kind of kid who gets picked on at school!"

Michael doubled over, as though he had been punched in the gut. A wimp? Had his father called him a wimp? But he'd heard it, hadn't he?

He turned and staggered back to the campfire, without waiting to hear Cil's response. She would, no doubt, defend the wimp.

He stopped just outside the circle of light thrown by the fire and straightened up slowly.

His father had washed him out of the boat on purpose. That was what he'd meant when he'd said he was going to "catch an eddy." And he, Michael Ostrom, was just about as dumb as anyone could possibly be. Here he'd thought his father had saved him — the way Cil had saved his father — when Bert Hensley was the one who had risked his life in the first place!

And he didn't care what anybody said about that stretch of river being safe; it hadn't felt safe. It had felt like dying. Exactly.

If he was a wimp, there was a name for his father, too. His father was a bully . . . and of the worst kind. The kind who snuck around and did things behind your back so you wouldn't know what had been done to you, wouldn't realize he was the one doing it. Like getting him to skin that jackrabbit, gut it, cook it. Like getting him to eat that stinking rabbit when he knew all along it wasn't good for eating.

Like telling him not to hang on and then washing him out of the raft!

Tomorrow the whole group was going through the Royal Gorge. Everybody said it was the toughest commercially rafted white water in the state. And yet he was going through it with the man who had dumped him out of the raft just to see him swim. Just to see him scared!

Well, he might be a wimp, but at least he wasn't that dumb. He knew enough not to hand a bully a second chance. Not when he had any kind of choice left, anyway. The rest of them might be going through the Royal Gorge. But they were in for a little surprise when morning came. Every one of them. They would find out that the wimp had a mind of his own.

No more "don't-hang-onto-the-rope, I'll-tell-you-when-to-paddle" swims for him! Because he wasn't getting back into that raft again. Ever!

Michael moved closer to the fire, on the side farthest from the trainees, and squatted there. A long stick was lying on the ground. He picked it up and poked the fire with it. Sparks rose in a shower of light, faded, and sifted back to the ground as feathery ash.

He sat, holding the end of the stick into the fire, waiting. For his father to return so Michael could confront him? For his own rage to turn to ash? He wasn't certain. He knew only that this man he had centered his life on, even through all the years of absence, had failed him. Yet again.

Why, Dave would have known better than to scare the life out of someone as a test. Dave wouldn't have called him a wimp, either. He wouldn't have called Michael anything, for that matter.

Michael sat, holding himself together like shattered

glass, studying the tip of the stick burning in the fire. When his father and Cil returned, however, he said nothing, did nothing. Just went on gazing at the flames. His father sorted through the gear and dropped a rolled sleeping bag on the ground beside him.

"Here's your bed, son," he said, and Michael nodded, still staring at the fire. He couldn't have looked at the man if his life had depended on it.

But Bert Hensley didn't wait for any kind of response. He went to gather his own sleeping bag, and he and Cil made their way to the far side of the campsite, off behind a couple of large boulders. They seemed to have made up their little quarrel.

Soon the last of the trainees had settled, too, calling good night to one another and to Michael, who didn't bother to reply. The stick he held into the fire was green and burned slowly.

After everyone had gone silent, he withdrew it from the fire and held it against his shoulder, aiming its smoldering tip in the direction of the boulders.

"Pow!" he whispered.

Once more the firecrackers filled Michael's dream. They kept popping and banging and wouldn't stop. He was alone, riding the booming rapids, and it was impossible to tell if the explosions came from the river itself or from inside the raft.

The raft spun, danced toward a whirlpool, and Michael paddled frantically against the sucking pull.

But then the paddle erupted, too, another infernal firecracker, and his hands were empty. The river reached up to grab him.

The force of the last explosion had been blinding, deafening, and yet nothing could prevent him from seeing the water closing over his head, from hearing the ring of his father's laughter as he was pulled down.

But then the dream changed. He had been waiting for the change, hoping for it. Now he was standing, rising out of the river, moving on top of the water, even. He no longer held the traitorous paddle. What he had in his hands instead was a .22, semiautomatic rifle, and he was firing it. Pow! Pow, pow, pow!

Someone was laughing, but the laughter ended abruptly the first time he pulled the trigger.

Michael found himself sitting up in his sleeping bag next to the cooling remnants of the campfire. The night sky was filled with stars, each one achingly clear, and the people sleeping around him were indistinct, dark lumps.

Only this time, unlike the other times he'd had the dream, he wasn't crying when he woke up.

· 15 ·

It wasn't his fault, was it, that the dream kept coming
back? Michael picked up the stick, still lying there
from the night before, and stirred the dampened
remains of the morning's campfire. Or his fault, either,
that his father had turned out to be a jerk?

Everyone was bustling, gathering for the day's run,
but Michael paid no attention to the buzz of activity. He
sat on the ground, hunched over the sodden ashes.

What would Bert Hensley say when he told him? *I'm
not going. It doesn't matter what you want, what you tell me to
do.*

Maybe he would respect Michael for refusing, after
all. Hadn't he been the one to ask why Michael had *let*
Neil Hansen bully him?

But then, did he really want the man's respect?

"It's time to go, Mike," his father called over his
shoulder as he passed, carrying a pair of oars. "Get a
move on, will you?"

Michael pressed his knee into the stick, meaning to
break it, but the slender branch only bent. He tossed it
aside. "I'm not going," he called back. His mouth was
dry, but his voice came out clear and strong.

Bert Hensley stopped, completely and abruptly, as if he had come suddenly to the end of a restraining rope. He turned until he faced Michael, his eyes squinting against the early morning sunlight.

"What did you say?"

"I said I'm not getting into the raft. I'm not going with you today." Michael didn't get up from the ground, but he straightened his back and jutted his chin. The man wanted tough; he would give him tough.

His father's eyes narrowed further. His mouth disappeared into a tight, straight line. He laid the oars on the ground, moving with the meticulous care of someone who chooses to put down something that he is tempted to throw, and walked back toward Michael.

"Would you like to explain?" he asked, his manner too steady, too reasonable.

"There's nothing to explain. I'm just not going."

His father was standing very close to where Michael sat, towering over him. Michael could feel his nearness, like the presence of an animal of uncertain temperament.

"Chalk it up to me being a wimp," Michael added, waiting with something close to satisfaction for the attack that was sure to come. He could defend himself. Everyone would be surprised at how well he could defend himself.

Cil was observing from the background. She had moved closer, but not close enough to interfere. Several of the trainees had stopped what they were doing as well, and they watched from a respectful distance.

But his father didn't move. "You were listening," he said, still without emphasis or inflection. "You were eavesdropping last night, weren't you?"

"No." Michael shook his head. "I was coming to get you . . . to ask where my sleeping bag was. That's all. And I . . . heard."

His father said nothing, neither to accuse further nor to try to explain. There seemed to be a kind of blank between them, the same blank there had been for the last eight years.

"You washed me out of the raft on purpose." Michael could hear the heavy calm of his own words. It might have been someone else speaking. The calm didn't come from his own rapidly beating heart, that was for sure.

"You're right, son," his father replied. "I did."

Michael hadn't expected the stark honesty of this answer, and he didn't know how to respond. After riffling through his mind without finding anything that seemed to be of use, he decided to leave the next move to his father.

The silence hung there between them. It was like a glass dome over the entire camp. More and more of the trainees had come to a halt on the periphery of a tenuous circle, watching, waiting.

Cil came toward them. "Mike," she said, "I know how you feel, and I don't blame you. But you weren't hurt.

Your dad wouldn't have put you in any real danger, you know."

Michael neither looked at Cil nor answered her. None of this had anything to do with her. Besides, she was doing no more than repeating his father's argument from the night before, and even if it was true, it changed nothing.

"What will you do," Bert Hensley asked, still perfectly calm, "if you don't finish the trip?"

The question caught Michael in the gut. How stupid he had been, not to have made some kind of plan! He had been so busy thinking about opposing his father, about protecting himself from the man's "tests," that he hadn't once thought what he would do instead. Only that he wouldn't go.

So he said the first thing that came to his mind. "I'll hike to the road," he indicated with a nod the highway that followed the river on the other side, "and hitch a ride."

"A ride?" his father repeated, his voice ripe with innocent surprise. "And just where will you hitch a ride to?"

Michael was caught — he knew that — and his fury grew. Where was there for him to go but back to the trailer, to his father's trailer? The man knew that.

Since there was no point in answering the question, he clamped his jaw shut and said nothing.

"I guess it comes down to this." Bert Hensley's voice was more forceful now. He seemed to be speaking for the benefit of everyone who was listening. "You can hitch a ride if you like. But if that's what you choose, you'd better plan to keep on going. All the way back to your cows in Minnesota."

Michael glared. Curiously, his first inclination was to defend the cows! But before he could open his mouth, he realized they were, of course, beside the point.

Still, he couldn't go back to the farm. There was no question about that. It would be the worst kind of defeat, to come slinking home admitting what everyone there knew . . . that his father didn't want him, that his father had never wanted him.

All of which would mean that Bert Hensley had won . . . again. Winning was easy if you didn't care. You just left when you wanted to leave. You dumped people when you wanted to dump them.

Only he, Michael, was through being dumped.

Whether his father wanted him or not, whether his father could be trusted or not, Michael was here, and here he was going to stay until he damn well decided for himself that he wanted to be somewhere else.

Without a word, he stood up, walked to the raft, and climbed in.

"Good boy," Cil said softly as Michael passed, but he ignored her. He ignored, too, the whispered comments exchanged by some of the trainees . . . and his father's victorious smile.

Let the man smile now, while he could, because sooner or later that smile would be wiped away.

Michael didn't know how exactly, but he was going to do it.

The cliffs of the Royal Gorge contained the water's roar, enclosed it, bounced it back at the occupants of the tiny raft. The rock walls rose so high on either side of the river that the sky was only a narrow blue strip far above. And though the atmosphere between the three people on the boat was heavy, with only the most necessary words being spoken, the buoyant raft shot past one obstacle after another as though charmed.

"This one's called The Grateful Dead," his father called at one point to no one in particular. "After you go through it, you're either grateful or you're . . ." He left his sentence dangling, and Michael saw Cil, who was rowing through the gorge under his father's supervision, flash him an irritated look. But if she thought she was protecting Michael, she needn't have bothered.

He didn't need her protection . . . or anyone else's, for that matter. He was just waiting for his opportunity to get even, and he would recognize it when it came.

This must be how men fight wars, he said to himself. *They get so they don't care about anybody, especially themselves.*

Strange to think that Dave had fought a war and that his father hadn't. Beneath all his silence, if you let yourself see, you knew Dave cared . . . for the farm, for his mom and Kari. Dave might even have cared for him if he had given him a chance.

Though it was too late to think about that now. Years too late.

Early in the afternoon, they pulled all three rafts to the side, climbed a shifting bank of shale, and balanced across an old water pipe to scout Sunshine, a seven-foot falls. Without even a tremor, Michael looked across and down on the falls they would soon be going over. He could feel his father watching him, and he returned the look with a directness and blankness that made Bert Hensley, after a moment, turn his own gaze away.

After they had piled back into the raft, his father called to the trainees, "Anybody who's not scared here doesn't belong on the river."

I belong here as much as you do, Michael said to himself. *You'll see.*

He set his jaw, gripped his paddle, and faced into the roaring drop.

Cil guided the raft over the falls as smoothly as if Sunshine were only a water slide, and followed closely by the trainees, they sailed through the succeeding rapids without incident as well. When they were tossing among the rocks below Royal Gorge Park, where the "wannabees" gawked at them from observation decks, Cil and his father gave the audience a wave. Michael didn't even look up.

But then they were faced with another rapid. It wasn't much, really, not nearly as bad as many they had already been through. Neither Cil nor his father had even bothered to give this one a name. Their entrance into the rough water wasn't quite as smooth as usual, however, and Cil was shouting, "Back stroke! Back stroke!"

Before Michael had time to do more than dip his paddle once, the raft came up against a rock hard, on his side, and stopped there, caught, tipping crazily. They were going to go over!

Instantly Cil changed her command to "HIGH SIDE!"

Michael could feel his father moving toward him, scrambling, grabbing, lurching up the slippery raft. For a fraction of an instant, Michael was immobilized. The man was coming at him, and he wanted to push him off, to send him back all the miles, all the years. But he was frozen into place.

And then, without ever having made a conscious decision, Michael found himself turning, and he was moving too . . . up and away. He was reaching for something solid, something that wasn't tipping, falling.

Now he had it. His hands seized hold of their own accord, pulling his body after them. And when he looked back over his shoulder, the whites of his father's eyes were gleaming like distant stars.

It wasn't until he could no longer see the bright terror in his father's face that he realized the "something solid" he had taken hold of had been the rock itself, and that he was perched on it, alone, in the midst of the foaming water.

Without the ballast of his weight, the entire boat had described a graceful arc, and his father and Cil had fallen free. The two of them, fragile looking in the river froth, careened between the rocks, bouncing off of them, being sucked under water, reappearing again, moving away from him. Away.

Michael clung to the rock, calling after them. "Ha!" he yelled. "Ha! That's for you!"

And then without pause, he was screaming, yelling at the top of his lungs, though he knew, even in this terrible moment, that his words were entirely foolish.

"Daddy! Please! Don't leave me!"

But his father was gone. He had disappeared, pulled beneath the tumbling water, and Michael could no longer see him anywhere.

He could see Cil, her hair streaming out behind her, sodden and dark. She wasn't swimming exactly, but leaning back into her life vest, her feet pointing downstream. And then she slipped around a curve in the river, and she, too, was hidden from view.

Michael cried out again as the next raft shot past, but this time his call was only a wordless wail. When the final group of trainees went by, so close that he could almost have reached out and grabbed an oar, he merely stared into their astonished faces and made no sound at all. They shouted something back to him before they floated on, but he couldn't make out what it was. "Good-bye," he supposed. Just that.

Michael gathered his knees beneath his chin and settled himself on the ridge of the boulder. Though he was still partially dry, he was shivering violently.

Would Cil die? He had seen her thrown into a boulder when she had first been dumped from the raft. And his father, was he already dead?

Perhaps his dream had come true. Except he hadn't needed a gun to make it happen. The only thing he had needed was to be himself.

Michael Ostrom, the wimp.

Michael Ostrom, the killer.

The water thundered past him, enclosed him, cut him off from the rest of the world. Michael checked the riverbanks. They weren't more than twenty feet away on either side, but they might as well have been a mile. The force of the current would take and toss him like a twig if he tried to move from his perch. Exactly as it had taken Cil. Exactly as it had taken his father.

Michael buried his face in his arms, rocking, rocking. He felt as cold and hard, as dead inside, as the stone on which he sat.

· 16 ·

Michael sat, imprisoned by the river, clutching his knees to his chest. The dry surface of the rock that extended above the water was so small that he was unable to move in any direction. He barely had space to shift his weight, and his legs, his buttocks, the muscles that ran up his back were growing numb.

It didn't matter. Nothing would ever matter again.

He had killed his father. Even if he hadn't actually pushed him away, he had wanted to. Even if he hadn't meant to leave the raft, it's what he had done.

The raft never would have tipped if he had stayed in. His father's weight combined with his on the high side would have righted everything.

But now, even if his father was alive, there would be no way to face the man again. No way to face himself . . . ever again.

If only he had stayed behind. He had known since last night it was the wrong thing, coming on this run. He should have hiked up to the road and hitched back to the trailer instead. Hitched anywhere, it wouldn't have mattered where.

Maybe the trainees would save his father — and Cil

too, of course. Or maybe the two of them would have floated into calmer water downstream and made their own way to shore. But even if they did, there was no way that he, Michael, could be saved. No way! Oh, he could be pulled off this rock he had climbed onto, but he couldn't be returned to his life . . . to any part of it.

He had ruined everything at home with Dave. He had spent years ruining it. And now he had done the same with his father.

Michael pressed his knees into his eye sockets, shutting out everything except the roaring of the water all around him, except the death-cold spray of the water. He wanted never to see another human being. He wanted to slip off of this rock and disappear, to go under the way he had yesterday. Only this time he wouldn't come up again. He would make sure he didn't come up again.

Michael had removed his life vest and was holding it in his hands when the trainees appeared around a distant bend in the river. They were walking, spread out along the riverbank, heading his way. He watched for a few moments and then, slowly, put the vest on again. So he was going to be rescued, whether he wanted to be or not.

When he saw Cil, towering in their midst, and his father at her side, a sudden relief burned through him. They were alive! Both of them! But the relief passed, leaving his mouth tasting of ash. What right did he have to be glad? What right?

The group stopped just across from the rock where

Michael waited, and he could see that one side of Cil's face was scraped and bloody. His father showed no visible injury, but he didn't even glance in Michael's direction as he spoke to the others, apparently giving orders.

That was all right. It was better, really. Michael didn't want to look at him, either.

Two of the trainees walked upstream, carrying what looked like a heavy bag attached to a rope. One anchored the end of the rope by sitting and holding it. The other indicated to Michael, signaling across the deafening clamor of the rapids, that he should be prepared to catch.

Michael readied himself as best as he could, turning toward his rescuers . . . away from the near bank where his father stood. On the first toss, the bag fell short. On the second, Michael watched it slip through his hands as though the hands belonged to someone else. When that happened the trainees all shouted a wordless groan of dismay.

The third time the bag passed over Michael's head, and he caught the rope, grabbed on somehow, and allowed himself to be pulled off the rock into the pounding river. The frigid water stole his breath, pummeling him, attacking him from every side.

Now, Michael thought. *Now let go*. But even as he gave himself the order, he knew he wouldn't do it. In fact, without even wanting to, he clung with all his strength to the slender rope dragging him through the water.

For a heart-stopping moment, he ricocheted off a boulder and went under entirely, but he came up sputtering. His rescuers pulled the rope in steadily, hand over hand. When he could stand, finally, and take the last few steps to the grassy bank, he was certain he had been battered bloody. On stepping out of the water and inspecting himself, he was almost disappointed to find nothing that ran red.

Everyone was talking at once, but Michael couldn't attend to any of it. Cil ran to greet him, talking, too. She pulled him to her in a fierce hug, and he stood there, dripping, his face turned away from the embrace.

His father walked up beside Cil. He waited until she had released Michael, almost guiltily, and stepped back.

For an instant Michael thought he saw relief in his father's eyes, a trace of gladness that his son was safe, that they all were. However, when Bert Hensley spoke, there was neither relief nor gladness in his voice.

"That," he said, "was the act of a coward. Abandoning a boat in dangerous water is the most despicable thing a man can do on the river. You could have gotten Cil and me killed."

After which he turned and walked away.

Michael watched him go. He wanted to shout after him, "I did it on purpose. Just like you did to me!"

But he knew it wasn't true. He might have liked himself better if it had been.

Michael sat on the couch in the trailer, wrapped in a blanket, his teeth chattering crazily.

"Are you all right?" Cil asked again, and again Michael stared at her wordlessly.

"Mike, answer me," she commanded.

And so he did, though he hadn't known what he was going to say until he heard himself say it. "I want to go home," he told her. "Tomorrow."

Cil sat down on the other end of the couch, tugging on a corner of the blanket to cover him more fully. The welt on the side of her face wasn't bleeding anymore, but it was turning purple and swelling. Her right eye had taken on an exotic, almost oriental look.

"Give your father time," she pleaded. "He'll get over being angry."

Michael shook his head. That wasn't the point, but he wasn't quite sure what the point was.

He wished Cil would leave. There was no need for her to stay on and play mother. She could go see what her boyfriend was doing, for starters, see why he had hung around his truck settling and resettling the gear instead of following them into the trailer.

"Mike, professional boatmen have done what you did there. All of us, we live in terror of just such a moment. Whether we mean to or not, we're afraid we'll save ourselves someday at the expense of our raft."

She laid one hand on his shoulder, and he shrugged it off. She drew the hand back apologetically, but she went on talking, went on defending his father. "You're just a beginner. It was your first time out. When your dad's had time to think about it, he'll understand. Believe me."

Michael didn't believe her. He hunched down further into the blanket.

"It's just that on the river we trust one another with our very lives. Every minute. We have to. When something goes wrong, when someone chooses his own safety over yours and your fellows . . . well, feelings run high."

But he hadn't even chosen! That's what was so ridiculous about the whole thing, so terrible. Still, Michael couldn't think of anything more than what he had already said, and having said it once, the second time was easier. "Will you take me to the airport tomorrow?"

Cil sighed. "If you insist, of course I will. I'll call when I get back to my place, make sure we can get a reservation. Shall I call your mother, too, or do you want to come with me and talk to her?"

"You call her, please." The idea of speaking to his mother — or even worse, to Dave — made his teeth chatter more violently. What could he say? *I've made a mistake — my whole life has been a mistake — but even so, I want to come home.*

Cil stood. "I wish you would reconsider, Mike."

He said, "No," and she sighed once again, though why the whole thing should bother her, Michael couldn't figure. Surely she didn't need a kid here causing problems between her and Bert Hensley.

"I'd better leave so you can get into dry clothes." Cil reached as though to touch him again, to run her fingers through his hair perhaps, but then she withdrew her hand once more. "I'll go home and make the calls and be back in the morning. I'll take you to the airport then . . . if you're still determined to go."

Michael tried to thank her, but the words caught in his throat.

She stepped to the trailer door. Then she paused, turning back slowly. "Let me tell you something about your father," she said.

Michael waited.

She examined him closely before she spoke. She seemed to be trying to judge his readiness for her message. "He loves you," she announced finally, and Michael couldn't help it. He let out a rude snort. It sounded exactly like something his mother would say about Dave. Why did women always talk about *love* when they came up against men's failures, as though the mere word explained everything else away?

Ignoring his rudeness, Cil went on. "Sometimes he doesn't know how to show it, though. Mostly, I guess you could say he's scared."

"Scared?" Michael sat up, the word startled from his mouth.

"I mean it." She shrugged. "That's why he has to act so tough all the time. That's why he needs you to be tough, too. He thinks the world's a pretty dangerous place, and I suppose he's afraid you'll get swallowed up somehow."

Always running. That's what Sam had said, but Michael hadn't wanted to hear that . . . or what it implied. His eyes wandered from Cil's gentle, wounded face to the mass of flame-colored hair, dry now and tumbling about her shoulders. "What's he got to be afraid of?" he demanded to know.

She gave him a small, weary smile. "You and me, for starters," she replied.

And Michael snorted again, because that didn't make sense. No sense at all. How could anybody on earth be afraid of him . . . or of Cil, for that matter?

It made him remember a time when he had said to Dave, trying for some kind of connection, "It must have taken a lot of courage, being a soldier in Vietnam." And Dave had answered, in his unsatisfactory way, "Sometimes it takes more just to face the cows every morning."

"Or to face the people you love," his mother had added.

Michael hadn't understood any of it . . . then. He wasn't sure he wanted to understand it now.

Cil stepped out of the trailer and closed the door.

Michael heard her exchange a few words with his father. (So he had been out there all along.) And then the motor of her Volkswagen beetle coughed into life. After she had driven away, his father came into the trailer.

His expression hadn't changed, however. It was stiff, unforgiving — certainly not scared, whatever Cil said.

"I'm going home tomorrow," Michael announced. It was the first time he had addressed Bert Hensley since his rescue — actually since their argument that morning — and suddenly he knew, quite desperately, what he wanted. He wanted his father to say that he couldn't go, that he wouldn't let him run away. To say that running was no way for a man to live.

But he replied only, "I figured that's what you'd want." And then he set about making supper. He worked at it steadily, as though supper were the most important thing in the world, much more important than Michael's decision to leave.

He fixed grilled cheese sandwiches and canned tomato soup.

Michael changed into dry clothes and began to pack his suitcase, which still stood next to the couch, while he waited for the food. It didn't seem as though he should be hungry, but he was. In fact, he found himself wanting to ask if there was any sweet pickle relish. He liked sweet pickle relish in a grilled cheese sandwich, spread on the cheese before it began to melt the way his mother always fixed it. He didn't ask, though. His father probably didn't have sweet pickle relish, anyway.

When they had finished supper, Michael thought of offering to wash the dishes, but he didn't do that either. There was little enough to wash, and besides, it was a little late for friendly gestures.

It took only a few more minutes to finish his packing. It was mostly a matter of moving his still-folded clothes from the drawer to the suitcase. Then he sat at the table in the tiny trailer, staring out the window. Night was pressing in as though the mountains themselves were moving closer.

When Michael finally spoke, his voice was too loud in the small space. "Why'd you invite me?" he asked, his jaw set as he waited for a response. "Why'd you call after so many years?"

His father had taken a clean towel from beneath the sink, and he was polishing each dish and pan and spoon dry before putting it away. He answered without looking at Michael. "I thought it was time," he said, which was no answer at all.

"Time for what?" Michael persisted.

His father didn't reply. He put away the last dish, wiped the sink itself dry, shook out the dish towel, and hung it over a cupboard door. Then he came and sat down on the other side of the table.

"I guess we've disappointed one another pretty badly in the last couple of days, haven't we?" he said. The unflickering light of the kerosene lantern on the table bleached his face of color and expression, too.

Michael shrugged, looked away.

"Cil warned me," his father continued. "She said I ought to think about it more before I called — about what I was trying to do, slamming back into your life that way. She said it wasn't fair, me letting some other man raise my son through all those young years and then trying to take him back, just when he was getting to be a man."

A man? Michael almost laughed.

"I guess she was right, as usual. Women often are, you know. About us, I mean."

Michael nodded automatically.

"But still, there's a piece she never understood. It

wasn't me just wanting to play the hero, to cash in on some other man's investment. It's more that I wanted . . ."

He hesitated, and Michael held his breath. He was going to find out something. He didn't know what, but something important.

When his father began talking again, however, he seemed to have shifted to a different track. "I've moved around a lot. I suppose I won't stick with the rafting more than another year or so."

Or with Cil, Michael realized sadly. And it *was* sad. He had a feeling Cil was one of the best things that had ever come to his father. A better fit for him than Michael's mother had been, certainly.

"I don't know if you'll understand any of this. You're pretty young." His father went silent, as though there was nothing more to say.

Michael leaned across the table. "Try me." He spoke quietly, but it was almost a command.

His father flashed him a surprised look. "Well," he said at last, after another silence in which he sat examining his calloused hands as though the words he wanted might be found there, "my life was beginning to feel . . . sort of temporary, I guess you could say. When you finish a run on the river, it's done. You know? So I guess I found myself thinking about you. A lot. Not just now and then the way I used to."

Not just now and then! Michael felt that along his spine. So during all the years he had carried this man in his heart, constantly, day and night — all the "conversations" they'd had — Bert Hensley hadn't been thinking of him equally. Only *now and then*.

"I found I liked the idea that some part of me was following behind, would be staying when I'm gone. At least for a time. I wanted to know who you were." He looked Michael full in the face for the first time. "That's all."

And now you know, Michael thought. *And it doesn't help, does it?* He stood, but then he realized there was no place to go.

His father stood, too, picking up the lantern as he did. "It's been a rough day . . . for both of us. I guess we'd better turn in." He held the lantern low, and the light, cast upward from his hands, threw his eyes into shadow so that his face took on the outlines of a skull. Except that a skull wouldn't have shown creases of fatigue . . . and disappointment.

The man blew out the lantern, set it beneath the cupboard, and moved in the sudden darkness toward his bed at the end of the trailer. The curtain rings sang along the rod as he jerked the curtain back, but then there was silence.

Michael waited.

"Michael," his father said finally, using the proper name for the first time. He hesitated once more so that the name seemed to hang there, waiting, too. Then he said, "I'm sorry."

Still Michael didn't move. Surely there would be something more! But his father only sat down on the bed and pulled the curtain closed.

He hadn't bothered to say what he was sorry for. For calling Michael a coward? For leaving him so many years before? Or sorry, perhaps, to have come to know him at all?

Michael made his way to the couch and sat down gingerly. He felt fragile, like a husk that might crumble at too strong a touch. After a few minutes he heard his father get into his own bed, and Michael lay down without bothering to undress or to climb into his sleeping bag.

The moon was apparently at the wrong angle to illuminate the little trailer, or perhaps it hadn't risen from behind the mountains yet. The darkness was so complete that, as Michael lay there, he couldn't make out even the .22 rifle propped above him on the wall.

More to confirm that the gun was still in place than for any other reason, he sat up, ran his fingers along the smooth length of it, and then eased the rifle off the pegs into his hands. The weight of it, the power of the weapon filled him. But after a long, silent moment, he knelt on the couch and returned it to its place.

It wasn't his. He had lost his own gun.

As he had lost everything else.

· 17 ·

"You don't have to go, you know," his father said as Michael settled his suitcase into the back seat of Cil's car.

Michael looked at his father helplessly. They both knew that he did. What good did it do to start pretending now?

Not that things would be any better back in Minnesota. Just that it was impossible to stay on here. "I guess they need me at home," Michael said. "There's always lots to do in the summer."

"And in the fall and the winter and the spring," his father added, trying on a chuckle that slipped immediately away. "Don't let the old man work you too hard, Mike."

The old man. The one his father had given him over to . . . and then tried to take him back from. And now was ready to return him to again, whatever he said about his not having to go. What he didn't realize was that Michael didn't belong to Dave, either, that he had never allowed himself to belong.

"Thanks, anyway," Michael said. "And . . . and I'm sorry, too. About yesterday, I mean." About everything.

About not being any kind of help for his father's "temporary" feeling. About being who he was.

"Yeah," his father said, running his fingers through his hair. "Well, things happen. You know?"

Cil was standing back, as though she thought, left to themselves these last few moments, they would work something out. Michael could have told her how useless it was. Women might understand lots of things, the way his father said, but they didn't seem to have a clue about the chasm between fathers and sons.

Even now, Michael thought, *you could* ask *me to stay. That might make a difference. If you asked like you really meant it.*

But his father didn't ask; Michael had known he wouldn't.

They shook hands before Michael climbed into the car. Like two men. Like two frightened men.

When Michael stepped inside the gate at the Minneapolis–St. Paul airport, he saw Dave standing just outside the barrier . . . alone. Michael came to a halt so suddenly that someone bumped into him from behind. It was a harried-looking businessman who readjusted his pace and hurried on, grumbling to himself.

So his mother had sent Dave to meet him. For an instant Michael was angry. Why did she keep doing that? And then for another instant, he found himself actually wondering . . . might it be possible to talk to Dave, to tell him what had happened? To start over with the man?

Michael approached shyly.

"Are you okay, then, Michael?" Dave asked, his gaze searching Michael's face for a brief instant before fleeing to something on the other side of the big room.

"Yeah . . . sure," Michael found himself replying, his voice filled with the old sullenness, though he hadn't meant it to come out that way. And the moment was gone.

Dave nodded. Apparently Michael's answer was what he had wanted. Certainly, it was all he had expected.

What had made Michael think Dave might have been interested, anyway?

The two of them walked in silence to the baggage claim area, sat in silence over a supper hamburger at McDonald's, drove in silence home. Nothing had changed. Nothing ever would.

Dave made a few comments about the state of the fields they passed, about the work waiting on the farm. Michael didn't respond, however — what was the point? — and Dave soon gave up the unnatural effort. Michael leaned back in the seat and watched the lush, familiar land and the sun, squashed and red, settling behind the greening fields. He ached for something he couldn't name.

For a father? For a man who would neither test nor ignore him? For some change in himself? One that would make him acceptable? Especially to himself. He sighed. It would never happen. None of it would ever happen.

His mother was waiting at home, and Kari. Kari had

been at a friend's birthday party. Mom had stayed behind to deliver her and bring her home again . . . and to do the evening chores. That was the excuse, anyway, for Dave's coming alone to get him.

Michael knew the real reason was that his mother had been maneuvering to give him and Dave time alone together. She was always doing that, setting things up so the two of them would have what somebody in a magazine had labeled "quality time." If she could ever let herself see how little good it did, surely she would have given up long ago.

But then maybe she wouldn't have. She wasn't the kind of woman who easily gave up what she wanted. If she had been, she wouldn't have managed to keep this farm, running it alone after her widowed father died in a tractor accident while she was still in college. Running it alone again after Michael's father left.

Kari watched Michael warily, as though he might have changed in his few days away. Mom was quieter than usual, too. She didn't hover. She didn't even ask how his visit to his father had gone. That was too obvious, he supposed. She just gave him a quick hug and said, "It's good to have you home, Michael." Then she went back to stirring the aromatic kettle of strawberry preserves that was bubbling on the stove.

"I'm pretty tired," Michael said, after standing awkwardly in the middle of the kitchen for a few moments. "I guess I'll go to bed."

"Good idea," his mother replied, pushing her dark, silky hair out of her eyes and smiling at him. And then she added, as though she thought it would help some-how, "How about French toast and fresh strawberry preserves for breakfast?"

"Great!" Michael said, but though he had meant to be enthusiastic, the answer came out sounding feeble.

He unpacked his suitcase slowly, putting everything in its place. When he came back from 4-H camp, he usually left his suitcase lying in the middle of his floor, using what he needed out of it until his mother nagged him to take care of things. It seemed important this time to eliminate every reminder of his journey. He even carried his dirty clothes to the bathroom and dropped them down the chute. He had been gone such a short time, he hadn't had reason to discover what his dad did about laundry.

Maybe Cil did it.

No. She didn't seem like the kind of woman who would hang around to do a man's laundry, though Michael couldn't help wondering, just a bit, why she hung around at all. *He's scared*, she had said, in the same neutral way she might have said, *He has a cold*. As though that excused anything.

Michael's first mistake had been telling his father about Neil Hansen. He should have told him instead that his son was a jock, quarterback on the junior high football team, the toughest, most popular guy in school.

Even if his father had been foolish enough to believe him, would it have felt any better, though, to have the man like him for a lie?

It was a meaningless question, because Bert Hensley probably wouldn't have liked him anyway, no matter how many lies he had told, no matter how hard he had tried. And there wouldn't be another chance. His father would move on to a different job — wrestling grizzly bears, maybe. He would put that old trailer down briefly in some other spot, and he wouldn't bother to call again, certainly not with an invitation to visit.

Michael turned off his light and started toward the bed, his eyes adjusting, even as he moved, to the bleached light from the now-full moon that sifted into his room. Halfway across the room, he paused in front of the mirror. He could make out his own image clearly enough. He was small, compact, dark . . . like his father.

He stepped closer. His eyes were hard to make out, but he knew they were the same hazel, not-quite-green, not-quite-brown color as his dad's. And his mouth had a discontented set that reminded him of his father as well. Maybe all this time he had been looking for the man in the wrong place. His father was in the mirror all right, had been all along. But he wasn't hidden in some remote recess. He was right there in Michael himself.

His mother and Dave had come upstairs, and now he could hear them in the next room, their bedroom.

"You have to talk to him," Mom was saying. "You can see he's hurting. He's just screaming hurt."

Dave gave a reply that Michael couldn't make out, his voice rumbling and low. *Why should I care?* That's what he was probably saying. *He's not my son.*

His mother responded to whatever it was he had said in a harsh, angry whisper. "It's not the same, coming from me. He needs a father. He needs you! Can't you see? Sometimes I could just kill Bert Hensley for . . ." And then she must have turned away because the rest of her words dissolved into an indistinguishable murmur.

Kill? His kindly mother? Michael wanted to laugh. Almost. But then he found himself caught with another idea. His mother and Dave were fighting . . . over him. Was Dave going to leave, too?

Dave was answering, his voice still calm and low so that Michael couldn't make it out. He put his face closer to the mirror. Maybe the words would come clear on the other side. But of course, they didn't. He had passed through to the other side, the way he had always wanted to do, and nothing had come clear. If anything, it was all more muddled.

"You men!" his mother replied to whatever Dave had said, speaking even more forcefully than before. "You and Michael both! One as bad as the other. You act like somebody's going to take you by force if you open the door a crack." And then he could hear the lamp click off, the bedsprings squeak . . . and silence.

Apparently Dave hadn't responded to that last accusation. *You men!* Said with disgust. *You men*, including him, too.

But he wasn't a man, and he knew that even if his mother didn't. Mothers were blind about some things. And despite being fed up with her husband right now, she must realize Dave was better than her son. Whatever she was talking about, he had to be.

Michael moved silently to his own bed. He had never felt like such a failure, poison to everyone he touched. Even Kari must have seen it when he had walked in, the way she held back, that cautious watching.

Maybe she could see it in his face somehow, his cowardice. She had probably seen it before now, when he couldn't even shoot a lousy pigeon, when she had gone and done it for him.

He punched an indentation in the pillow and dropped his head into it, face down so that he had to hold himself rigid in order to continue to breathe.

Somewhere in this house there was a gun put away. His gun, which had been given to him and then taken back again.

As soon as he got a chance he was going to look for it, find it, make it his own once more. It wasn't that he still thought having a .22 rifle could change any of the things that mattered. If you were a shrimp and a coward without a gun, you'd be the same with one. And you couldn't use it to make people like you, either.

But the gun was his, after all. And the idea of possessing it again made him feel . . . like there were still some choices left.

· 18 ·

Michael opened his eyes, and the clock on his bedside table came into focus — 7:48.

He sat up. He had slept through chores. He had forgotten to set his alarm last night, and he had slept right through.

Why hadn't Dave come in and wakened him . . . or his mother? Having managed without him for a few days, had they decided they didn't need him anymore? He stood up and grabbed for a pair of jeans. If he hurried, he could get out there before the milking was entirely done.

Then he sat down again. If they needed him, if they had wanted him, they would have come to get him. Wouldn't they? He stood again, more slowly this time, and began once more to dress. When he was finished, he went out into the hall.

The house was silent. Clearly, Kari was out helping with chores, too. It would be unlike her to be still sleeping. Michael paused at the door to his mother and Dave's bedroom. He seldom went in there anymore. He could remember treating his mother's room as an extension of his own when he was a little boy. She kept a small TV on her dresser, and sometimes they used to sit on the bed together in the evening, watching television.

Not since Dave had come, though. It wasn't that Dave had told him to stay out. He hadn't needed to; he was so big. It had always seemed that he took up all the extra space in his wife's room . . . in Michael's mother's life.

Michael stepped inside the bedroom and drew in a deep breath. The familiar fragrance of rose cologne lay on the air. No matter that she would be working in the barn or gardening or driving a tractor most of the day, his mother always dabbed cologne on her throat and the backs of her hands. Probably even "the ladies" recognized her by the scent of roses.

Michael opened the door of the closet and pushed through the hanging clothes. As he had expected, his .22 lay on the high shelf in the back. It wasn't even hidden behind anything. But then his mother and Dave hadn't expected him to be home so soon. Maybe they hadn't expected him to come home at all.

The cartridges were on the same shelf, just a little farther back. So Dave had violated one of the basic safety rules about storing a gun. Neither gun nor ammunition was locked up, and they had been stored together. Michael clucked his tongue as he pocketed a handful of cartridges.

Standing in the hallway, he loaded the clip, snapped it into the .22, and checked the safety. He worked methodically, not even concerning himself with the idea of being caught. If someone came in from the barn . . . what did it matter?

He paused, briefly, in the kitchen. A pastelike mass of oatmeal was cooking slowly in a double boiler. With raisins in it. He hated raisins. Obviously his mother had forgotten her promise of French toast.

It didn't matter. *He* didn't matter, really.

Michael stepped out into the quiet yard. A rope-and-board swing that had once been his and now was mostly Kari's hung motionless from the arm of a massive oak. A bee droned past, ignoring him. Not even Nipper came out to greet him. He must be at the barn with the others.

The .22 made a comfortable weight, balanced under his arm. Michael set out walking toward the hills.

He didn't know how long he had been walking, or how circuitous his route might have been when he stumbled into the clearing and discovered the tree with its rough platform. Almost as though the rifle had led him to the place.

It was the stand he and his father had used the time they had gone deer hunting. Michael was certain that was what it was. There were short boards nailed into the tree trunk to form steps, and above, a crisscross of further boards made the platform from which they had looked down upon the deer.

Tucking the .22 securely beneath one arm, Michael climbed to the platform. It was, as everything else seemed to be, smaller than he had remembered. He supposed the buck they had killed that day, if he could see it now, would be smaller as well. He settled with his back against the trunk of the tree, the rifle propped on his knees, and looked out through the rustling screen of leaves.

Cicadas buzzed. A swamp in the valley below rang with a steady chorus of peepers. Michael listened as though he might detect some kind of message from the clamor, but if there was one there, it wasn't intended for him.

A monarch butterfly, orange and black, zigzagged past his perch, and he followed it through the scope. He didn't fire, however. It wasn't a varmint. If he killed it, he would have to gut and skin and eat it. The thought brought a twisted smile.

A squirrel scolded and racketed from a neighboring tree. The noisiest animals in the woods, squirrels. For a few moments Michael held this one in his sights. It was a small red, its tail almost as vibrant and alive as Cil's hair.

He turned the gun away. What was the use? What was the use of anything?

He sat so still for so long that after a time he imagined he could see the buck he and his father had shot, see it again as though it had walked once more into the clearing. Its great rack of antlers high, ears alert. The leathery-looking nostrils working the air. The eyes dark, soft.

And then the buck was down, and his father was

standing between him and their kill, blood steaming on his hands. The bloody hands, the fallen buck seen through the blur of his own tears.

"What's the matter, son?" his father was saying. "Santa's got lots of reindeer. He won't miss just one." And then the laughter, as penetrating as the knife that had drawn the deer's dark blood.

Was that how it had gone? Had his father been the one to suggest that it was Santa's reindeer they had killed? Had he been trying to "toughen the kid up," even then? As though a five-year-old boy needed to be prepared for a life of slain reindeer?

Possibly. He would never know for sure.

If that's the way it had been, it would make sense of the small boy's picking up a dead branch and attacking. The branch smashing again and again against the curved back, against the bloody hands that grabbed at him, smearing him. Staining him.

He'd been a pretty brave little kid to go after his father that way. Not just to want to, but to really do it. Too bad he hadn't finished the job.

Like in the dream.

Like in the dream where he finished everyone off.

Neil Hansen, his face as bland as a peeled potato, as without thought as a potato, too.

All the other Neanderthals who taunted and tormented.

Mr. Warner, the principal, who ran a school where bullies could stuff firecrackers into pockets and run off home for the summer, unscathed.

The teachers, at least those who stood by and didn't interfere.

No. All the teachers. There had never been anyone left at the end. No one who had stood up for him. No one who tried to stop him.

Not Gary or Chris.

Not Dave. Especially not Dave.

Or Kari.

Or his mother.

All of them gone. Wiped out. And Michael standing alone, a thin, blue wisp of smoke curling from the barrel of his gun.

He looked down at the rifle cradled in his arms and touched the warm drops he discovered there, dark against the polished metal. Strange. He was crying, and he hadn't known. Crying for everyone, for everything he had destroyed.

Because he was the problem, he alone. Not his father. Not Dave.

Sometimes I could just kill Bert Hensley, his mother had said, his gentle mother. But which Bert Hensley did she want to kill? The one she saw in her son?

She would never be able to do what needed to be done, though. Not in a million years. He, Michael, was the only one who could do it. The only one.

With shaking hands, Michael worked the bolt, sliding a cartridge into the chamber. He clicked off the safety and turned the rifle until the barrel rested against his right cheek. He made each move slowly, methodically, with deliberation and care. And yet inside he was spinning out of control, his descent, he knew, already begun.

He gripped the stock between his sneakered feet to steady the rifle and stretched out an arm, reaching for the trigger.

And saw once more the downed buck, the pigeon, the jackrabbit, its front paws scrabbling horribly at the ground.

And heard his father laugh.

And knew that, at last, he had found a place where bullies couldn't reach, where even his father's disappointment couldn't touch him. Because it would all be over in an instant for him. Everything would be over. Even the fear.

He squeezed his eyes shut and stroked the smooth curve of the trigger, his father's laughter still ricocheting through his skull.

Only subtly changed and changing. This time it was the exuberant laugh with which Bert Hensley had greeted him when he first arrived at the trailer, the laugh that had come pouring from his father's throat as he had spun him around.

We've got to get to know one another all over again, don't we?

Michael brushed his cheek lightly against the cold barrel of the gun.

Was it so terrible that his father was afraid, that he was? Was it possible that everyone was afraid, everyone who was alive?

He touched his tongue to the rim, tasting gun-powder and metal, tasting death.

Tasting the end of his pain, the beginning of everyone else's.

His mother's.

His father's.

Dave's.

Kari's.

Cil's.

Even Neil Hansen's, who would never have a chance to forget the stupid little joke he had played.

The sweetness of the earth would be diminished for each one of them, because of him. Their lives made even more temporary because he had run away.

Carefully, slowly, Michael removed his hand from the trigger. He stared into the dark mouth of the barrel for a moment before separating his feet to release his hold on the gun. The rifle disappeared, sliding off the edge of the platform. When it struck the forest floor, it discharged. The sharp retort reverberated across the valley like thunder, and Michael shook with it.

He hadn't meant for the gun to go off. He was lucky not to have been hit. Lucky to be alive.

The silence that followed was so complete it was like the silence of the grave. But after a few moments the cicadas and the peepers resumed their song; the red squirrel scolded once more from a nearby tree.

Michael was limp, exhausted. As though he had been running for miles. As though he had been running for years. All the way to his father . . . and back again.

He didn't think he hated the man any longer for leaving him. It was possible he didn't even hate himself for being left. How could he? He had come face to face with himself these past days, with the worst he could know . . . and perhaps with the best as well. And nothing took more courage than that.

But he hadn't the additional strength to climb down from the tree, to pick up the gun, to walk home.

So he lay down where he was and waited. What he was waiting for, however, he couldn't have said.

Michael lay listening, his cheek pressed against the rough boards of the platform. Someone was approaching, crashing through the underbrush, moving clumsily and fast. How long it had been since the gun had gone off, he had no idea.

He pushed himself up against the trunk of the tree just in time to see Dave plunge into the clearing. His face was a mottled red, and he pulled at the air in great gasps.

So Dave knew where this place was, probably had known all along. Michael should have asked about it long ago.

Dave stopped, stared at the gun lying on the ground. The air, pouring through his throat, made a sound almost like sobbing.

"Michael," he called, stumbling toward the tree and looking up, but blindly.

Michael waited until Dave had time to climb the few

steps, to hoist himself over the side of the platform, before he answered, "I'm here," he said.

Dave reached for him, drew him close, crushed him against his chest.

Michael took a deep, wavering breath, filling himself with the man's musky warmth. Would he say it? *My son. My son.*

It didn't matter. Dave had come. Michael closed his eyes and rested in the silence.